Petro del Jarko 16

Savages Station

Savages Station

A CIVIL WAR TRIPTYCH

By

Pietro del Fabro

Lectori Salutem Press

www.savagesstation.com

Contents

Deep Love to Maria
my favorite rebel

Introduction

When I first went to Waterloo, New York, to design the American Civil War Memorial, I had no idea how immersed I would become in the lives of the fifty-eight men from the village who died in the war. I still remember my Civil War history professor reciting the roll call of the states seceding from the Union. A deep interest in the Civil War began, and so it was for over a decade after college. But things change, and in 1976 my focus shifted toward art and Italy. Perhaps the shift was a result of my college Latin courses or my marriage to an Italian woman. Over the next three decades my wife and I travelled to Italy over forty times. We read Italian novels, art history and cookbooks in an attempt to bring the life and taste of Florence, Montepulciano, Urbino and Ischia to our table. I sketched and painted my way through more masses in the great Italian churches than I can count. It was the ideal place to learn from the masters, but my interest in the Civil War faded.

In 2007, the design process began for the American Civil War Memorial. Out came my old Civil War books and a whole new life, filled with reenactors, archival research and travel to the battle sites and graves of the Waterloo veterans. I did not turn away from Italy but rather wove it into my designs. My concept for the memorial revolved around a cenotaph field. Each of the Waterloo fallen would have a limestone cenotaph carved by a local citizen. In addition, I proposed we create a series of short biographies. After extensive research at the National Archives and in village records and newspaper files we now have online a biography for each of Waterloo's Civil War fallen. Many discoveries called out for further development. I wanted to share all that we learned in our research, so I decided to write a triptych of stories (*Memorial Day, Savages Station, Cenotaph*) that would reveal to the modern reader little known aspects of the war interwoven with the contemporary story of the American Civil War Memorial. Although I have changed the names, each story springs from the lives and events we researched. The military events, places and major figures of the war are factual.

Part One

MEMORIAL DAY

Strange, what brings these past things
vividly back to us...
HARRIET BEECHER STOWE

May 26 - 2008

The artillery sergeant couldn't help but notice the woman. She was not only a stranger, but a beautiful one at that. His job was to supervise the cannon crew, to keep a careful eye on the loading of the black powder, but she captured his imagination and his attention wandered. In the searing heat of the late May afternoon she moved to the center of the ceremony with the cool grace of a prima ballerina, then knelt on one knee before the red flagpole. She looked up at the thirty-six-star flag, then rose and bowed her head. *Who would do that,* he thought, *kneel on freshly mown grass in a full length taffeta dress?* The deep blue fabric glowed in the bright light, releasing the crackling sounds that only silk can produce, the folds shifting and tightening against her limbs.

"Stand clear!" the sergeant snapped, as the gun crew prepared to fire. The woman looked toward the cannon. Others had already placed stones around the flagpole base, one for each of the thirty-six states of 1865. The Alabama Black Creek sandstone had been brought forward just before the stranger appeared. Now her moment had arrived to present the last stone, the South Carolina blue granite.

The sergeant stared at her. Something was different, but he couldn't place it. He was sure it wasn't just the way she walked or the elegant Civil War era dress and high top button up shoes, or even her luxurious long brown hair captured in a tight bun. Then he realized, it was her eyes. She had the languid eyelids of an Italian Renaissance Madonna, a face that belonged in a Raphael triptych.

It was a perfect Memorial Day in the Finger Lakes for the dedication of the American Civil War Memorial. Puffy cumulus clouds floated

3

high in a crystal azure sky. At least half of the audience was turned out in period dress of the Civil War era, and across the green, Union and Confederate reenactor regiments stood at attention. The memorial director tapped on the mike to check the sound system. "Can you all hear me?" He wore a plaid sport jacket, green chino slacks and spit-shined loafers. Old Ray-Ban aviator sunglasses seemed to cover half his face. The scratched lens caught the sun in odd ways, sending out scattered rays of multicolored light.

"Now, folks, before we place the last stone I want to introduce an important guest. Our first two stones came from Massachusetts and Iowa," the director's voice broke a little, "they were sent by Lieutenant Colonel Pete Shaw of Hingham, Massachusetts." He clenched his jaw then continued. "Colonel Shaw was a sergeant in the 28th Infantry Regiment, 8th Infantry Division, one of the units engaged in the Battle of the Bulge. Later his unit was involved in liberating the Wöbbelin concentration camp."

The director reached for a handkerchief in his coat pocket and wiped his brow. It was clear he didn't need to do that, he was stalling for time to compose himself. The colonel's past resonated with the director, himself a World War II veteran. He folded the white cloth, placed it on the lectern then turned back toward Colonel Shaw.

"Throughout his life the colonel has been actively involved in the VFW and American Legion, including service as past grand commander, Grand Pup Tent of Massachusetts." The director stopped again, struggling to keep his composure. He bit his lower lip. "Pete is one of my great American heroes. How about a hand for Colonel Shaw who is with us today." The audience broke into loud applause as the colonel rose. He was easy to spot with his white VFW commander's hat and black suit coat covered with campaign ribbons, sharpshooter medals and Combat Infantryman's Badge. The colonel waved, a bit surprised at the unexpected attention.

"Thank ya, Colonel," the director said, leaning forward into the mike. "Now, ma'am," he continued, turning toward the woman who had been all but forgotten, "we're ready to lay that final stone." He gestured with his left hand held out toward her. "The blue granite of South Caro-

4

lina is given in memory of Captain Thomas Wells, 5th Regiment, South Carolina Volunteer Infantry. The stone is presented by Mary Romulus."

The director stopped again to wipe his forehead, his face dripping with sweat. "Ladies and gentlemen, thank you for coming, this brings us to the end of our dedication ceremony." He motioned for Mary to continue, then gathered up his papers, stuffed them inside his coat and sat down behind the podium.

The woman had patiently kept her position before the flagpole. She made good use of the time to observe the artillery sergeant and noticed that he kept staring at her. *This will be easy,* she thought, *he seems to like me, he'll have no idea what he's in for.*

Mary knelt back down, both knees resting on the grass. She reached forward and placed the stone on the ground, then balanced back on her knees and hesitated, lost in thought, not sure what to do next. The sergeant turned back to watch. He was to fire the gun when the last stone was placed. It seemed she might never move but then she leaned forward, lowered her head and kissed the stone. What he could not see, from thirty yards away, were the tears in her eyes.

"Ready!" barked the sergeant, his right arm up. All he could think about were the grass stains on her dress. He imagined he could smell the damp green turf pressed against her knees. *Damn shame,* he thought. He turned to see her rise then bend down to touch the stone one last time.

"Prepare to fire!" The gun crew leaned away from the black barrel and covered their ears just as the woman took her seat.

"Fire!" shouted the sergeant, his arm moving down.

The concussion ripped through the humid air, startling the crowd. Then the sound of two trumpets floated across the island. The pure notes of taps worked their magic and everyone relaxed. With that the sergeant gave his last order of the day. "Clear the gun."

The woman stood, adjusted her dress, and walked toward the light artillery unit. She extended her hand to the sergeant who was surprised to meet the woman who had so recently captured his attention. "I'm Mary Romulus," she said in a soft voice.

The sergeant, a bit taken back, took her gloved hand and gave it a half shake. "It's my pleasure to meet you madam, I'm Sergeant Hopkins." He hesitated, then added, "It was beautiful, I mean the way you laid the stone." The smell of lavender floated in the air. The sergeant scratched his nose and picked up the scent of sachet left on his fingers from her glove.

"But you, sir, you had the hard work." To emphasize her sincerity, she placed her free hand on his shoulder and drew it down his arm. She was surprised how solid he was, how lean and muscular. In her experience American men, especially Northerners, tended to go flabby pretty fast after a certain age. The only sign of his years were the faint traces of crow's feet starting to work there way out from the corners of his eyes and a little bit of salt and pepper scattered through his neatly trimmed beard.

"Be mighty obliged, Mrs. Romulus, if..."

"No, Sergeant, you must call me Mary." Something in her voice seemed unexpected, mysterious, but he couldn't place it.

"Yes, Mary...Mary..." he stumbled. She had thrown him off his Civil War reenactor politeness, but he recovered quickly. "Yes, madam, would you be so kind as to stand over here with my squad for a picture?" He dug in his wool uniform and pulled out a small digital camera, then thrust it into the hands of his corporal before directing the woman where to stand. She moved with perfect posture among the soldiers who gave way to bring her in front of the gun.

"Now, Sergeant Hopkins, come stand by me, we must do this right." With that the squad lined up and the camera began to click. The sergeant proudly showed Mary the images on the little screen.

"You're quite the handsome man in a uniform now, aren't you, sir?" She was always surprised at how some people were so photogenic. Hopkins was a good-looking man but the photo enhanced the angular features of his face. The dark blue of his coat set off his tanned skin to perfection, while his above-average height gave him the command presence expected of a gunnery sergeant.

The men moved to prepare the cannon for departure. Mary stood back, then nodded her head toward a clump of lilac bushes. "Kind sir, may I have a word with you in private?" She held her hand out to direct him away from the men struggling to maneuver the gun back onto the road.

"Your soldiers move that cannon like it weighs nothing, Sergeant."

"The big wheels make it easier, it actually weighs almost half a ton."

"Mighty impressive noise it makes, sure scared the crowd."

"Yes, ma'am, it's an accurate copy of the 3-inch Ordnance Rifle of the Civil War. The originals were mostly made by the Phoenix Iron Company in Phoenixville, Pennsylvania." Her face went a little pale. He had seen it before when he carried on about his equipment. "Sorry, ma'am, technical stuff can be pretty boring." He pressed his hand to his heart, then added, "Now tell me, just how can I help you?"

She turned to face him under an oak tree beside the race that ran along the north edge of the island.

"The Regimental Cenotaph," the woman whispered.

"What did you say?"

"Look, just there, sir." She pointed behind him. "It's the Regimental Cenotaph."

He pivoted to the left and saw a large limestone stele, about seven feet tall with a broken top. Incised in the stone were the names of Civil War battles and New York regiments.

"Sir," she began, her gaze focused on him, "it has come down to me through several friends that you have a Southern branch in your family." He knew now what he had heard in her voice, she was a Southerner. He didn't reply, he wanted to hear more.

"Romulus is an upstate New York name as you must know, but after the war," she hesitated, then repeated, "after the war, and because of the war, most of my family moved south. The war pitted brother against brother...our family was deeply affected by the conflict."

"Ma'am, where..."

"Sergeant, I'd really be obliged if you'd call me Mary."

"Yes, as you've said...so Mary, where are you from?" He had family in Virginia, on his mother's side, and suspected that was what she wanted to talk about.

Mary looked away for a moment toward the men lowering the flag. "No one's in Virginia anymore, I know you have family there. I'm from South Carolina, a little town near Columbia that found itself in

7

the way of General Sherman when he came up from Savannah in sixty-five."

"That's a mighty long time ago for sure."

"Indeed, for some, especially you Yankees, but for us it seems mighty recent considering the outcome."

Sergeant Hopkins nodded. "My Virginia cousins still talk about the fighting as if they just saw it on the evening news."

"So what's it like down there in South Carolina these days?"

"You'd love it, y'all come down...oh my, I almost forgot!!" She reached into her purse. "Here, Sergeant, thank heavens you asked, I brought you this." She placed a small jar in his hand. "It's the best way to know our state, strawberry preserves from my garden! Think of me when you taste it."

"Very kind of you...Mary!"

"Our area is so beautiful, distant views of the mountains and some-times, early in the morning, we find a wild turkey or two picking through the strawberry patch." She hesitated, her eyes gleaming. "They're just looking for bugs, they wouldn't dare touch my strawberries!"

"I'll try your preserves on my toast in the morning, ma'am, it's sure to be a wonderful taste of your Carolina kitchen."

"Cooking is one of my specialties, Sergeant, you haven't lived 'til you've tasted my Southern fried chicken." She licked her lips and swallowed. "I use an Italian olive oil instead of lard, sprinkle on some hot pepper flakes to give it just a kiss of heat."

"You're making me hungry now, aren't you, Mary!" He pushed the jar into his pocket and looked back to see how his troops were doing. "I must go help my men, but first tell me, how might I be of service."

"I want you to go with me here..." She reached behind the sergeant and brushed her hand across the incised letters of a word on the Regi-mental Cenotaph. The perspiration on her glove left a dark smear on the limestone under the name of a battle. "I want you to go with me to Pennsylvania, to Gettysburg, in July." She looked for a reaction.

It wasn't so much what she asked but the directness of her request that caused him to pause. *This woman isn't wasting any time,* he thought, *knows what she wants.*

"Sergeant, you're familiar with some of the men from Waterloo, the brave New York soldiers we honored here today?" Her eyes narrowed. "Many were wounded, a few were killed on the fields below Cemetery Ridge."

"Yes, several fell there, one's even a cousin of my great-great-grandfather." He hesitated, looking toward his men. "I was just there last summer for an anniversary reenactment, it's awfully soon for me to return." He wanted to be polite, but he was a married man, why in heaven's name would he go off to Gettysburg with a female stranger?

"Sir, I know this must seem bold, even outrageous..." She took his hand and held it between her two gloved hands. "Please, Sergeant, this is of great importance to both of us."

The physical gesture felt warm and there was comfort in her touch. Maybe that turned his mind, the feel of the Southern woman, or maybe it was her moist eyes.

July 1 - Morning - 1863

Private James Wells knelt behind an oak stump, his rifle propped on the flat sawed top. An early morning shower had done little more than dampen the ground and push up the humidity. The sun sat low, no heat in the rays yet, but that would change. He chewed on a soggy biscuit and looked ahead into the woods off to the west where the enemy would come. He had never heard the rebel yell but the others had warned him. In fact, he had never done any of this before, he knew he wasn't thinking straight. Sleeping on the ground can confuse a man's mind. It had been a sticky damp night with rumbles of thunder in the distance. His sleep was filled with nightmares, especially a recurring one in which he was buried alive, wrapped in a blanket on a moonlit battlefield. Just before dawn he had removed his shoes to rub his itchy feet, then fallen back asleep with only his socks on.

When he woke at first light he realized he'd slept under a fig tree. He stared up into gray branches covered with deeply lobed leaves, but there was no fruit, the figs wouldn't be ready until August. A blue jay landed on a branch just above his face and sent bird droppings flying past his left ear. He jumped up cursing and stubbed his toe on a high root. His father's admonition came back to him: *Check your shoes for spiders and centipedes before you put them on.* When he went on overnight hunting trips his dad always gave him too much advice. Once he found a small garter snake in his shoe and held it out to his son to prove the point. That's exactly why Wells now put on his shoes without checking them. He took satisfaction in doing things his way. Surely his stinky feet would kill anything lurking inside.

A major walked out of the Seminary building and headed right for Private Wells. *About time,* he thought. He had been waiting for some direction ever since the 126th New York had detached him for duty with Buford's Cavalry. Bad enough to be going fresh into battle, but no one should have to go alone, who knows whose got a man's back when you're a stranger. To his left and right, cavalry troopers were tearing up fences to make breastworks. Wells didn't like anything about his situation. When the Reb infantry came, he knew it would be an unfair match—cavalry could not stop an infantry charge.

"This here's a perfect spot for ya, Private, they'll be coming soon." The major was covered in dust and smelled of tired horses. His scrunched-up eyes gave him a cranky look.

"How many we expecting, sir, only got cavalry on this line?" Wells spoke respectfully, but he wanted the man to know how wrong it looked.

"That's why you're here, son, to hold 'em down till our infantry can get up, might be noon before we're relieved."

Wells looked down and realized his pocket watch was gone. He tried to hold back his anger, but not too much, he knew it would mask his fear. "What time ya got Major, seems like a lotta time you all expecting us to hold on?"

"Seven-thirty son...we got at least an hour yet, scouts said their lead elements are still crossing the pike beyond Cashtown." The major looked away, wanted to change the subject, he knew what a mess they were in. "Fourth of July, be here in two days, can't hardly believe it. Where you from, Private?"

"Waterloo, sir, small village north of here in Western New York...I'm with the 126th." The major's eyes narrowed. Wells had made a mistake, he knew better. Early in the war the 126th had surrendered at Harper's Ferry and had been branded as cowards. It wasn't the men's fault, just bad leadership, but they had to live with it. "Reckon ya need me to pick off some Rebs when they step outta that tree line?"

"Not some, Private...lots! How fast ya shoot?"

"I'll be sending three of them Johnnies to St. Peter each minute!" Wells knew his abilities. He was the best squirrel and rabbit shot in Waterloo. He'd be missed in town. The stews wouldn't be so tasty this year.

The major looked him up and down. "That's an interesting weapon you got there, son, never seen a rifle with a hexagonal bore."

"It's a Whitworth, English made, got it off a dead Reb."

"What's your range, Private?"

Wells patted his rifle. "With this telescopic sight a Reb's dead at 1,500 yards, a .45 caliber bullet hits real hard."

"Three kills a minute, that's almost two hundred an hour, you got the ammo for that?"

"You keep the Rebs away from me, I got what I need."

"Were trying to keep them boys tied down long enough so our army can grab the high ground behind us in Gettysburg." The major liked the private's attitude, he reached out and patted Wells on the shoulder. "We want the Rebs to think we're infantry, to give them pause." The major winked then scratched his crotch. "You sting 'em good, son."

"I'll do what I say, Major, but the infantry better get here fast."

"Some regiments will arrive in a few hours but the main army, well..." the major paused, thought for a moment, "truth is, son, they're a day away."

Wells didn't like the sound of any of this. "Forgive me asking, Major, but I reckon the Confederates got a bunch of regiments gonna be walking out them woods?"

"Heth, son, it's Heth we're facing, one of Lee's best divisions. That's why we brought up you sharpshooters."

Wells pointed across the field toward the tree line. "Looks like it's about three hundred yards to the edge of that woods. Anyone comes outta them trees, you just tell me where you want the bullet." He tapped the long scope on his rifle to reassure the major. "I'm good, but those cavalry boys...just don't seem like ya have the muscle we need."

"Hear me good, Wells, I don't want ya wasting shots on the Reb troops, we've only got two horse brigades here."

"No disrespect meant, sir, but this seems like a suicide mission."

The major coughed up some phlegm then swallowed it. "Take out the officers, maybe you'll buy us some time, Private."

"Sir, I expect those'll be the one's mounted?"

The major cracked a smile. "Excellent, son, you'll do well. Shoot the riders but look for others, could be some dismounted officers with the troops. Shit, what's this?" The officer pulled up his sleeve, picked a tick off his arm and crushed it with his teeth. "So let's make it simple, Private, all ya gotta do is look for the Confederates with sabers. Reb officers love to show their metal, even whack a few stragglers with the flat of the blade to keep 'em moving." With that the major turned away and headed back. The smell of coffee and bacon hung in the air.

The morning had turned hotter but a mist lingered in the deepest part of the woods. A westerly wind filtering through the oak and hickory trees delivered a chilly breeze. The physical sensation of the unexpected coolness distracted Wells, lifted his spirit. He stood up to stretch his legs and look around. There was no comfort in what he found. The big guns the infantry counted on were absent. "Four hours," he mumbled, "no way we hold 'em for even two."

An artillery sergeant walked over and introduced himself. "This is where you be settling, Private," he began, then turned his head and spat a wad of chaw across the grass, "cause we want to keep our guns away from ya ass?" The gunner seemed younger than Wells, barely out of his teens, but his sunken eye sockets and mottled skin made him look much older.

"Yes, sir, Sergeant, this here's where the major placed me." Disdain burned in the sergeant's eyes. Wells had grown to expect this, it went with his green uniform. All sharpshooters wore a green coat and kepi instead of the standard Union blue, and all were marked men. Rebs and Yanks agreed on few things, but they both despised enemy sharpshooters only a bit more than their own.

The sergeant spat a stream of yellow liquid onto the stump. "You git yourself lots of gray coats, Private," he began, then laughed, "we'll feed some canister up their craw if ya miss any!"

"You boys gonna need more than canister to hold off what's coming!"

"Shit, what's the major been telling you, Private?"

"Says Heth's whole division is expected soon."

"Holy Jesus, I reckon that's all infantry!"

"Not gonna be pretty, Sergeant. I don't fear dying so much as being wounded...left to suffer. One of my best friends from Waterloo was deserted at Savages Station, Virginia last summer...his regiment abandoned him in a field hospital."

"They just left him?"

"Never been seen again...the Rebs overran the position."

"What unit?"

"33rd New York, his name was Fabrizio...Fabrizio Cenci of Company C...his mother and father were from Sicily, she was the best cook in town."

"Sorry to hear that, Private." The sergeant stared at Wells for a moment then rejoined his unit. Sounds of digging, stacking and talking filled the still air of the muggy July morning.

Wells expected no one else would approach; sharpshooters were to be avoided. "No way we hold off a whole division of Rebs," he whispered, then looked back to lay out a path of retreat. It was inevitable, he would have to move fast when the time came. The possibility of a desperate retreat frightened him, brought on waves of homesickness. He had no appetite, his stomach ached for home. *One friend,* he thought, *just one, and I'd feel whole again.* Off in the distance, beyond the fog shrouded hills to the south, his regiment approached, but the Rebs were coming faster. He pictured his comrades, tried to will them to run, but he knew it was no good, he'd be facing the onslaught with strangers today. Better get used to it.

He removed the cloth from his scope. The stump stood chest high, just right for steadying his rifle while giving full cover. Wells loved his weapon. He was glad he no longer had the standard Union issue Sharps Rifle. It was a decent carbine but not the best for precise killing beyond 500 yards. The Rebs didn't have much equipment that was better than the Yanks, but their English Whitworth stood apart as a superior weapon.

Wells squinted into the glass lens. The smell of the thin coat of oil on the barrel made his nose itch so he pinched it up high to hold back a sneeze. Two deer, a doe and a buck, jumped out of the woods. He moved the cross hairs onto the right shoulder of the male and began to pull the trigger, but held back at the last moment. *God knows,* he thought, *it could spook the cavalry and they'd all start shooting at nothing. Not the proper way to impress the Rebs. If you want the enemy to think you're infantry you have to act the part.*

He removed a flannel rag from his pocket, blew on the scope lens, then wiped it off. Wells scanned the tree line, then drew the scope closer to his eye for a better look. He caught a blurred motion, then the first Reb picket stepped out of the woods. An electric shock raced up his spine, his fingertips went numb.

Wells knew that blind fear can send a mind to crazy places; panic has ended many a battle before it began. Every Yankee on that line was well aware that they were outnumbered, knew that for the past two years the Rebs had pretty much had their way in the fighting. The Confederate infantry with their manic battle scream and fearless attacking style had turned more than a few Yankee regiments into mass confusion. It all began in 1861, at Bull Run, where the Yanks threw down their guns and ran all the way back to Washington.

Wells shifted his elbow to grasp the rifle tighter, to be sure he saw right. He rubbed his left eye, took a deep breath and looked again, but he had no doubt what the sudden quiet up and down the line meant. Only one Reb stood there, like a lost hunter in search of the deer he'd flushed out of the trees. The picket started to move forward. The soldier, dressed in a tattered gray jacket and black pants, moved with an easy confidence. And it was not the wild-eyed Reb he'd expected. The Confederate's cool demeanor shook Wells.

He lowered his rifle to get a wider view. More pickets stepped out of the forest gloom, twenty men spread out over a quarter mile front. The Reb uniforms were remarkable for their variety. Some had gray jackets, others wore butternut brown jackets with matching pants. A few had blue pants taken from dead Yankees. The only uniformity in their appearance was the blanket roll each wore over the shoulder and down across the chest.

"Let them come, don't fire," a lieutenant yelled down the line. The only sound Wells heard came from the men in blue fumbling for cartridges. He prayed the Rebs couldn't see this, they'd know for sure their opposition was only dismounted cavalry.

It's just a patrol, Wells prayed, *maybe nothing will happen here.* He scanned the forest edge, still murky in the early light. The Rebs stopped about half way across the field and knelt down, then a glint of metal flashed in the distance and the first infantry regiment stepped out in a straight line. Adrenaline coursed through his body, but it felt good, he was ready. He licked his forefinger and touched it to the tip of the rifle. "Just for good luck," he whispered, "bring the bastards on."

A solid wall of Confederates, perhaps two thousand, formed up behind the pickets and more regiments crept into view behind them like fog rolling across a harbor. It was quiet, no sound came across the field.

The Yanks looked frightened, fidgety. Wells was surprised to see how unsettled they were. There was none of the calm determination he had come to expect in the eyes of Union infantry awaiting a charge. The cavalrymen ducked lower behind the breastworks, as if they finally realized that the job of the Reb infantry was to destroy them.

Wells scanned the Reb lines as an officer on horseback emerged with the second line. He shifted his scope to bring the cross hairs onto the officer's stomach and waited. The rider talked to the troops as he moved up and down the line, reins firmly in hand. The Southern troops remained quiet and composed, the pickets kept down.

"Load solid shot and fire at will," a Union artillery officer shouted. "Change to double canister when they're at fifty yards." He charged down the line repeating his order as the Union artillery opened up. The Rebel guidons brought their colors to the full upright position and the infantry advanced. Wells could see the mounted Rebel officer waving back into the woods for more troops. It was then that the pickets stood and the manic yelling began.

"Fire low, make every shot count!" screamed the major. The first volley cut down half the pickets. The rest kneeled back down and waited for the main line of infantry to catch up. The Union artillery started to find its range and opened up holes in the advancing infantry.

"Steady," Wells whispered, "just keep coming." He squeezed off his first round, letting his breath out as the bullet left the chamber. He knew it was a perfect shot. The Reb officer jerked back, tried to grab the saddle horn but missed and flew over the tail of his horse and landed face down on the grass. Wells scanned to the right and found a new line of infantry moving out of the woods with four riders mixed in.

"Can't believe they do that," Wells shouted. His voice calmed him, kept his grip steady. "Look at 'em sitting up high…just plain stupid!" Four more precise shots, four more riders gone. "General Meade, lookie here," Wells screamed. "Maybe you should give all the troops Whitworth's and end this war right fast."

In answer, a minie ball slammed into the stump and sprayed him with splinters. "Son a bitch!" he hissed, then rubbed his eye to be sure he was all right. Wells looked up and saw two more regiments coming out of the woods. "Shit, Major, this ain't gonna last long!" He squeezed off another shot and watched a Reb officer grab at his chest then fall back, still in the stirrups, his horse circling slowly.

The fire grew in intensity, smoke everywhere, so much that Wells had a hard time sighting new targets. Acrid bursts of black powder burned his sinuses, made his eyes tear. The Rebs took lots of hits but kept coming, closing up gaps, moving forward. The screaming pitched higher, seemed like it might split his skull in two.

"You OK, son?" It was the major. There was blood on his hand and forearm.

"I'm good, sir." Wells moved to reach out and comfort the wounded officer but thought better of it. He turned back to adjust his sight. The Rebs were closer, it was almost at the point where he could aim down the barrel and forget the scope. Wells started to draw a bead on a red headed captain on a large tan horse when he heard a strange sound behind, like a muffled splash. It made no sense, he knew there was no stream or pond around. He rested his weapon on the stump and turned to look.

"Oh, sweet Jesus!" he screamed. An artillery round had neatly taken away the right side of the major's head. There was no sound, no cry of pain, he just fell to his knees and rolled down in a gushing pool of blood. The war had begun for Private Wells.

The tourists were thick as flies on a sticky bun. Bumper to bumper traffic clogged the road that circled the battlefield. Minivans, buses, SUV's, Winnebago's and Harley's were laid out in an endless line of idling machinery, all on the verge of overheating, and not a space left in the parking lots. It was no way to see Gettysburg, so early on the two visitors had agreed to walk. It was a sensible idea except that the high summer sun had heated the air to near 100 degrees, and they hadn't thought to bring water. The sergeant, who years before had done time in the real infantry, knew something had to change.

"Madam," he began, stopping to wipe his forehead, "we've got to get us some water or we'll end up buried out here like a bunch of Reb sappers."

"Look over there!" She hadn't heard a word he said.

"Where?"

"Over there by the parking area." She pointed to a bunch of bored adolescents tossing a Frisbee between cars along the battlefield perimeter road.

"They should be careful, might hit a driver in the head." The sergeant wasn't pleased. Just then one of the teens missed a catch and the plastic disk smacked into a man's head, but it wasn't a driver, it was the bronze head of General Lee sitting on his horse atop the Virginia Monument. The Frisbee hit the head with a loud report sending pigeons and bird droppings flying.

"Hey, how about showing some respect," the sergeant screamed but he was too far away for them to hear him. They just laughed and kept on playing.

"I'm impressed, sir!"

"Impressed?"

"Yes, sergeant, never seen a Yankee defending our General Lee."

"Damn kids today don't respect anything! Look at 'em, they'd just as soon knock Grant's head off as Lee's, probably don't even know what side he was on."

"Good for you, Sergeant, I'm sure you'd like to teach them a thing or two!"

"Be a waste of time, I bet. Anyway, ma'am, we best be moving along, I don't see any water around here."

"You're taking good care of me, Sergeant, I'm mighty obliged." She scanned the landscape for any sign of a rest room or concession stand.

"Mrs. Romulus," he asked, "perhaps..." but she cut him off.

"Remember, just Mary, none of that ma'am and Mrs. stuff, Sergeant." She was disappointed with his silly reenactor formalities. The Yankee meant well but she wasn't accustomed to his type of man. Mary treasured the complex, romantic, even ornery male of the South. She was sure everything had come too easily for the Yankee victors, it made the later generations soft, superficial and dull. Like most Northern men, the sergeant had not tasted the enduring pain of defeat, he was just a nice, boring guy.

"Now, Sergeant, I think we should head over to the right near the Seminary, there's sure to be a store there to buy some water, maybe a sandwich."

It was noon and the sergeant couldn't wait to get out of the sun. What he didn't know was that his companion was moving him exactly where she wanted. Hot day or not, they were headed to the Seminary.

"That's it over there, I believe..." The sergeant pointed toward a cupola that rose above the trees in the distance. "Maybe a ten-minute walk." He was glad he hadn't worn his wool Civil War uniform, couldn't imagine spending a summer campaign in it. A hot breeze blew across the grass and kicked up dandelion puffs. He raised the collar on his red Lacoste shirt to shield his neck from the burning rays. In the distance, to the north, low green mountains filled the horizon, reminding him of the vineyard covered hills that plunge into the frigid waters of Seneca Lake back home.

Mary stopped to dab the perspiration off her forearms. "Death is a difficult subject, Sergeant."

"Yes, ma'am...I mean Mary," he stumbled, "we're surrounded with it here...death I mean. Every time I come to Gettysburg I marvel at the monuments, there must be more stone markers here than any other place in America."

"How many died, Sergeant?"

"Eight thousand in three days, but that doesn't fully describe it, there were over forty thousand casualties and many died later." He slapped at a dragonfly on his sleeve. "The two armies brought a hundred and sixty-five thousand men into battle and nearly a third of them went down." He shook his head then looked up. "Imagine the scene in the days after the fight...and that's not to mention all the Reb prisoners marched away to suffer and die in Northern prisons."

"It pains me deeply, what happened here."

He wasn't sure what she was getting at. His eyes wandered up, high over the battlefield where two contrails crossed, luminous in the hot sky.

"Sometimes I weep, sometimes there are simply no tears left."

"Forgive me, Mary, but are you talking about the men who died here? It was so long ago."

"Our losses live a long time, Sergeant, the memory never seems to end." Mary put her hand against his back and directed him forward toward the Seminary. "I've brought you here so you can touch the war, the real war you spend so much time reenacting."

"I've touched it, Mary." She looked into his eyes, surprised at his response. "I spent time in Petersburg several years ago and went to the town cemetery to look at the Confederate graves. Down the hill, on the lower right side, I came upon a limestone marker with a jar of jam resting on the grass in front of it. It was strawberry jam just like the jar you gave me. At first I thought someone had left it by mistake after a picnic, but then I read the stone. It was an officer's grave, I think he was a major, and it spoke about how loved he was, how he had been given the nickname Jam by his troops." He stopped to be sure she understood. "Imagine, Mary, people been leaving a fresh jar of jam there all these years." She smiled, asked him what he did next. "I picked up the jar and saw it was homemade." The sergeant took Mary's hand as if it were the jar. "Even had the date penned in script on the label... so yes, Mary, I've touched the war."

Just then a cloud blocked the sun, covering them in its cool shadow. "Can't imagine it," he whispered, the back of his shirt now dark with sweat.

"What did you say?"

"Can't imagine living and fighting in these conditions for three days."

The heat was having its way with the sergeant. "Better be some water up ahead or..." He stopped abruptly in mid-sentence, surprised by the appearance of a young woman who stepped out from behind a boxwood hedge. She was a pretty sight, her starched blue poplin dress set off by the orange brick of the Seminary building shimmering behind her in the distance. His nose filled with the distinctive earthy fragrance of the boxwood's tiny leaves.

"Sergeant Hopkins, I'm Sally." The new woman moved in front of him, then held out her hand. He wasn't sure whether to shake or kiss it.

"Madam, I'm sure you must be from a Southern place, I can hear it in your voice...but my name...how'd you know?"

"Well, kind sir, I've been waiting for you."

Sally was as handsome a young woman as the sergeant had ever seen. Her straight black hair was cut above the shoulders. Bangs covered her forehead; olive green eyes and tan skin completed the picture. He raised her hand and kissed it. Her hand was a vision of femininity, the flesh cool, the nails meticulously cut and polished. Hopkins was quite embarrassed when she in turn took his hands. His fingers and knuckles were chapped and sweaty, his nails dirty and in need of a good clipping.

"Mary has been so kind to bring you here." She let his hands go and stepped back. The sergeant was mesmerized, every melodious word she spoke oozed Southern charm.

"There is a story to tell," she said, "then you can judge." Sally and Mary had agonized over how much to tell the sergeant before he came to Gettysburg. In the end they decided that silence was best; they didn't want to scare him off.

"Well, you have certainly brought me a great surprise..." said the sergeant in his politest tone, "please...do begin."

He remained gracious, but his chopped discourse betrayed discomfort. The heat of the midday sun seemed to have silenced everything, even the birds. It was as if time had moved back, as if the battle were about to begin–that moment when all creatures flee or hide in anticipation of the coming human madness.

"Look there, the view across the field towards Herr's Ridge. It's where the Rebs appeared on July 1, the first day of the battle. The Yanks were set up here on McPherson's Ridge..." Sally paused to point back toward the old religious buildings. "They had the Seminary at their back. The large building over there is where they brought General Reynolds when he was mortally wounded."

"Honestly, ladies, I feel bad...to disappoint you, but..." He stumbled searching for the right explanation. "You see...truth is...I'm just not familiar with this part of Gettysburg. If the first day of the battle is what interests you...I'm the wrong person." He began to turn away but thought better of it, tried to change the subject. "Sally, where do you come from, it must have been a long journey?"

"South Carolina, Sergeant, small town near Greenville, it's in the back of the state near the mountains." Sally's eyes lost their focus, she looked away.

"You're relatives, Sergeant," whispered Mary.

"My relatives," replied the sergeant, "what about them?"

"No, not your relatives! I'm sorry we are confusing you, I mean you are relatives...you and Sally." It was a moment of revelation. Mary and Sally waited for him to take it in.

"What relative..." he began, but didn't know how to proceed.

"Come..." motioned Sally. "Sit over here in the shade." She led him toward a stone bench under an unusual broad leafed tree of medium height. It was covered with odd-shaped, small green fruit.

Sally smiled. "I reckon you've never seen a fig before kind sir, too cold in Western New York for a Mediterranean tree." She tore a leaf off a low branch and handed it to him. "In South Carolina, even here in Pennsylvania, near the Mason-Dixon Line, they do just fine. If we come back in late August the fruit will be ripe, the dark purple skin cracked and swollen."

The sergeant, a religious man, looked up into the tree. "The only fig I ever heard of is Eve's fig leaf...you know, the one she covered herself with." He blushed. "To tell the truth, I can't remember if the apple or the fig leaf came first...in Genesis, I mean?"

"Sergeant, we've brought you here to ask your opinion, not to have a Bible lesson." Her tone changed. "We need to settle a family matter."

"So what's this all about?" he asked, but Sally put her finger to her lips to silence him.

"As Mary said, we are cousins and it is a sad story but perhaps you can lighten our pain...if only a little." The sergeant looked into Mary's eyes. She looked as if she might cry.

"There were two brothers from Waterloo, Thomas and James Wells who went off to war...but not together. James joined the 126th New York while Thomas moved south and ended up on the Confederate side," Mary said, tapping Hopkins on the sleeve, "but, imagine this, your great-great-grandfather was the rebel Thomas Wells, mine was James who fought on the Union side."

"Is that what I came all this way to hear, that I'm descended from a Reb?" Wells reached out to flick a wasp off Mary's shoulder. "I've heard there was a Reb way back in our family, but two brothers on opposing sides, that's new to me." He looked away for a moment at a motorcycle making a racket in the distance, then turned back. "You should know that in Waterloo we talk about our Union fathers, not the enemy. I'm not just a reenactor, I'm also a member of the Sons of Union Veterans."

"Sergeant, we assumed you were aware of your kin."

"What's next," the sergeant quipped, then laughed nervously, "perhaps you'll tell me I'm related to Stonewall Jackson?"

Mary took Hopkins by the hand and looked him in the eye. "James killed Thomas...do you understand what I'm saying, Sergeant?"

"How could that be?" The sergeant hesitated, scratched his elbow, "I would have heard...it's just not possible."

"Private James Wells was a sharpshooter, he killed his brother here at Gettysburg." Mary gave him a pat on the back then held him by the shoulders. "It was at very close range, James called out to Thomas just before he shot him."

None of this made sense to the sergeant. "Mary, you must slow down, it was long ago...how can you be sure?"

Mary shook her head to fight back tears, then nodded to Sally to take up the story.

"Thomas was a captain, a company commander in the rebel infantry. His men saw the whole thing, brothers meeting on the field of battle...only one surviving. The story's in the regimental records, some still talk of it, such things are not easily forgotten." Sally paused for a moment to hold Mary's hand. "It's the truth, Sergeant, but not the worst of it."

"I'm sorry, Sally, deeply sorry, I had no idea..."

"Imagine, Sergeant, that this happened in your lifetime, then perhaps you would feel the pain." Again, the sergeant apologized, but Sally didn't think he meant it. "Sergeant, would it change things if I told you that your grandfather Edward killed Mary's grandfather in 1985 when you were fifteen?"

"Now wait a darn minute...my grandfather killed a man, but it was an accident, a tragic mistake during a family hunting trip in the Blue Ridge Mountains." Wells always had doubts about the story, maybe it was different than his parents had told him. He was a child then, they may have shielded him. He looked into Sally's eyes and knew she spoke the truth.

"Oliver, the man he killed, was the grandchild of James Wells."

"I can't imagine...my grandfather loved me, I called him Eddie."

"Your grandfather killed James Wells's grandson. Perhaps the Civil War doesn't seem so long ago now, Sergeant?"

"I remember the morning...my mother told me her father had been involved in a hunting accident. It was the first day of summer vacation, late morning just after the mailman came...I was still in bed," he paused for a moment trying to remember her words, "she was upset, said it was a mistake."

"It was no accident, sir, it was direct revenge for the shooting of Thomas Wells at Gettysburg." Her sweet demeanor was gone. "Sergeant, do you understand, Mary lost her grandfather, murdered to avenge the death of Thomas Wells?"

Hopkins felt the full force of the heat, remembered how thirsty he was, wished he hadn't come to Gettysburg. "I can hardly believe what you're saying...how long ago was it?"

"In 1985, only a few years ago."

"Over a century after the battle...why?"

"Death cuts deep, especially when the killer is a brother," said Mary in barely a whisper, "the pain was still alive for Edward."

"Can't imagine killing a man because of something that happened so long ago."

"Our family never recovered from the loss of Thomas. His widow lived only a few years longer. She broke her leg trying to plow the overgrown cornfields and died of a hemorrhage a week later. Her son Billy, left destitute and parentless, took to stealing and violence to survive. In and out of jail for the rest of his life he somehow managed to have a son..." Mary hesitated.

"Tell him, for God's sake!" said Sally.

Mary looked around for a place to sit and settled for a nearby tree stump. "It pains me to tell you, Sergeant...Billy never married, his only child was born of a prostitute...his name was Edward, Eddie as you know him." She paused to let the sergeant understand.

"Edward somehow survived the impoverished and hateful world of his outlaw father, but the damage had been done. Stories of the Civil War filled his young head and too often he heard the story of James killing his grandfather. Eddie was nearly killed himself when the bounty hunters came to take his father. The bullet that smashed through his father's brain came to rest in Edward's femur."

"I know none of this." The sergeant grabbed onto a low branch of an oak sapling to steady himself.

"At the same time as Edward's family was descending into a vortex of violence and hate, my family prospered. James Wells returned to Waterloo after the war and lived to see his grandchildren educated at the best schools. My grandfather, Oliver, became a surgeon."

"It's too much," whispered the sergeant, "too much to believe."

"Well then," Sally interjected, "imagine what happened when the long lost cousins came together for the first time at the family reunion in 1985. Oliver was so pleased to meet his Southern family, he had no idea the hell they had lived through. It didn't take long for Edward to find his moment. Perhaps there was too much talk of our family success, or maybe it was just the alcohol, but Edward, in one quick moment, saw his opportunity deep in the woods...an "accidental" shot evened up years of suffering."

"That's outright murder...you did nothing?"

"There was nothing to be done, as you know your Eddie died of a massive stroke a week later."

"I don't know what to say." The sergeant rubbed his eyes, as if that might clear things up.

"Think of it this way, Sergeant..." Sally paused to be sure she had his attention, "it would all have been different if Thomas had lived."

"Yes, but..."

Sally frowned. "I'm mighty displeased with your responses, Sergeant, you have nothing better to say?"

"Tell me, sir," said Mary, "when's the last time you felt upset about the Civil War, about losing a relative in battle?"

"Look, Mary, I have no strong feelings about the war." He hesitated for a moment. "The truth is the conflict isn't something I feel bad about, in fact it makes me feel good, I reenact the winning side."

"Well, now that's a truthful reply." Mary looked relieved, a weak smile crossed her face. "Victors forget fast, don't they? It's not important to Northerners in the same way, that's why you're having a hard time understanding what your grandpa did...losers hold their pain close."

"This is all crazy...killing and more killing...what do you want of me?"

"I loved my grandfather," whispered Mary, "not a day goes by..."

"Mother, we mustn't blame the sergeant, just ask him what we've come here for and let him be on his way."

"My God," said Hopkins, "Sally is your daughter?"

"Well of course, who else would be here?"

"Can't make sense of..."

"Listen, Sergeant, just listen!" Mary snapped, then pointed ahead. "Over there, it's where James Wells stood the morning of July 1, 1863, waiting for the first Rebs to show their faces. I've brought you here because you are blood, we're all the same family, each one of us descended from two brothers who met on this ground."

The sergeant felt light-headed, he needed water, fast. "I believe you Mary…I truly know nothing of this." He was just mouthing words, couldn't think straight, but the women didn't see it.

"It doesn't matter a bit, I know you're no history person, but you're blood, that's why you're here." Mary walked a little forward to a small rise in the ground and pointed across the fields. "Way out there, Sergeant, past the creek is Herr's Ridge, take a good look, try to imagine."

"Imagine?"

"Yes, Sergeant, imagine your brother is out there." Mary paused, unable to say the next words. She didn't bite her lip like a man would. Instead, she waited until her jaw stopped quivering. "Or your grandfather."

"I wasn't here in 1863, I've never been here."

"You're not hearing me, Sergeant, I want to know what you feel, not what you remember." She shook her head then clenched her fists. "What is the matter with you, don't you see…our Civil War ancestor killed his brother? Can't you see our family is all torn up?"

The sergeant looked down. "I do feel bad, especially for you, Mary."

Sally reached out for his hand. "We don't want to know how you feel about James killing Thomas, that's done with." She paused and looked over to Mary for a moment then continued. "Would you kill your brother, Sergeant?"

"What kind of question is that?"

"We want to understand, Sergeant, you're the only one who might make sense of this family tragedy." Mary put her arm around Sally. "Please, we need to know what you would have done, tell us what a man, a fighter would do."

"How can I do that?"

"You're family, you're a reenactor," whispered Sally, "you put yourself in the shoes of a Civil War fighter all the time, it's what you do. Help us, Sergeant."

"Look out to the west," said Mary, "look at that tree line, close your eyes, imagine it's the summer of 1863."

The sergeant needed water, just wanted to lie down and cool off.

"Your brother is coming to kill you, doesn't know who you are, you're just the enemy to him. But, you know…you know it's your brother, you see him in your scope…" She paused to let the words sink in. "You don't want this, it's hard enough to kill a stranger…"

"For goodness' sake, Mary." He tried to play out the idea, suffering with the choice. He turned quickly, desperate for a drink. The harsh sun had dehydrated him. "Water, please, I need a drink…help me…" Just then a mosquito bit his face a little below the temple, and he slapped at it. That little bit of violence, and the blood on his hand from the flattened insect, started a panic attack. His mind raced, his heart skipped, he held his breath. "Please…some water…"

He tried again to answer the woman, but he fell to his knees, rocked forward and vomited. In the midst of disorientation he felt a hand on his shoulder. Sally reached out and wiped his face. He sat up, put his hands flat on the ground.

"Sergeant, look at me," said Mary. She poked him hard on the chest. "Your brother is coming straight at you, only you know who he is. It's kill or be killed, you or your brother…"

He stared up into the searing turquoise sky, his clothes soaked in cold sweat. "I'm making a damn fool of myself down here ain't I?" He reached out to Sally, pulled himself up. "It's kill or be killed, that's the choice you offer me?"

Mary pulled back a little to give the sergeant space to steady himself. "Kill or be killed, what do you say?"

The sergeant looked at her expression and saw arrogance for the first time. Beneath the Southern charm lurked a coldness that her words had hidden, but not her eyes. His moment of weakness had turned her. He realized she disdained all Yankees, not just him. Her eyes were dark with contempt for the Northern cause, for the injustice of the Union victory, for the perceived inferiority of the South. His fall had brought it all to the surface.

Perhaps it was better this way, he thought, *no pretense.* "You offer me a choice, Mary?" Just then a string of firecrackers exploded in the distance, the percussive sound echoing off the Seminary buildings. The sergeant looked away for a moment, then fixed his gaze back on Mary. "You brought me here thinking there was a military answer to your grief, that I could turn the riddle of brotherly love and death. I could have answered it just as well in Waterloo."

Her eyes narrowed, she licked her lips. "Kill or be killed, what do..." But he cut her off.

"My brother will live."

"Private Wel.....!" The burst of an outgoing artillery round cut off the word.

"Private!"

Wells started to line up his sights on another rider, brushed his finger down the curved edge of the trigger, floated the cross hairs just below the officer's shoulders, began to slowly exhale while bringing his finger back easy on the trigger.

"Wells! Private Wells!!"

He wasn't hearing. Wells was locked in the visual prison of his prey's destruction. The Reb's muslin shirt exploded, blood poured out, half his chest still cotton white, the rest red. The officer slapped desperately where the round went through as if that would make the problem go away.

"You hear me, Private!?" A big hand grabbed at Wells's elbow. "Let's go, Private, you're done here!" Wells tried to catch his breath, he was focused on the Reb. It was the second hand on his shoulder that caught his attention. He jumped back.

"Easy, Private."

"Sir!"

The lieutenant returned Wells's salute. "Report over there, Private, you're going with Baxter's Brigade." He pointed toward an infantry unit forming up between the Seminary buildings. "The Second Division is just coming up, I'm sure you'll be happy to get back with the infantry."

"Sir, yes sir."

"Report to General Baxter's adjutant, they'll be needing some of your type over there..." The lieutenant looked down when he said it, didn't mean to insult the sharpshooter. "He's the officer on the black horse."

Wells didn't look at the lieutenant, just picked up his gear, slung his Whitworth and moved off the line. "Enough of this cavalry nonsense," he whispered, "can't believe the Rebs haven't figured it out."

"Guess you're Private Wells," said the adjutant, "we're putting you with the 11th Pennsylvania, they'll need some long range shooting when Rodes gets here, he's leading Lee's largest division."

Wells froze when he heard the name Rodes. Private Wells's brother had moved to North Carolina five years before and in 1861 had written to announce his intention to join the insurrection. It was only recently he learned his brother Thomas was a captain in Rode's Division. He loved his baby brother, couldn't picture him fighting for the Confederates. Thomas was the family favorite, a sweet man admired by everyone in Waterloo. James had been the hunter, the marksman in town, while Thomas was the brilliant student who tutored all the school kids. James wouldn't have passed geometry without him.

"You all right, Private?" the adjutant asked, "you look distracted, maybe too much shooting for ya?"

"I'll be fine, sir, just point me to the Pennsylvania Regiment." He was far from fine. James felt dead inside, an emptiness crept into his bones, he could not imagine facing his brother.

"Over there, see that blue flag, Private?"

Wells saluted and started to move out.

"Hold up, son, here are your orders." The officer bent down and handed Wells a handwritten note. It was then he saw that the officer had only one ear. The right side of his head was covered with scar tissue, only a hole remained where his ear had been. "Report to Lieutenant Colonel Coulter...good luck, Private, we're counting on ya."

A commotion started in the distance. "Reynolds been shot!" called out a sergeant from a doorway in the main Seminary building.

"Jesus, no!" hissed the adjutant. He galloped off, leaving Wells alone in the midst of the turmoil. It was fine with him, gave him a moment to think, collect himself. A corporal ran by and Wells grabbed his arm.

"Who's Reynolds?"

The corporal barely stopped to answer. "General Reynolds, I Corps commander, he's d..." Wells couldn't make out the rest over the rumble of the artillery.

He asked for Colonel Coulter and a major directed him down the line to a group of officers kneeling on the ground. "Sir, Private Wells reporting as directed." He held out the note. The men looked up, each one focused on his green coat.

"You the sharpshooter the adjutant told us about?" asked a tall captain. He snatched the note out of Wells's hand, read it, then crumpled it into a little ball and threw it down. His pants were covered in mud that had dried into dark crackled layers that clung to his knees. The captain's jacket hung open revealing a torn white cotton blouse soiled a greasy yellow. He returned Wells's salute, then reached out to shake hands. The captain's fingers were stained with nicotine, his nails in need of cleaning. The officer was surprised at how cold the private's hand was on such a hot day. He started to say something, then changed his mind and pointed to the left, "The colonel wants you with Company C, I'll take you over in a moment."

Wells waited while the officers finished coordinating their assignments. They scratched troop movements in the dirt with bayonets. "Here..." began the captain, dragging a long steel blade across the ground, "this is Oak Ridge, just across the Chambersburg Pike." He pointed with his bayonet toward the north. "We've been asked to extend our line to the right. I'm told we'll be able to make it up there through some woods and here," he scratched a line along part of the ridge, "right here we should have a stone wall for cover. OK then, let's move!" The captain motioned Wells to follow.

"Is it Rode's Division we're expecting, sir?"

"All five brigades, son, I hope you're as good as I've heard." He lifted his hat and scratched the top of his ear. A crusty scab caught the edge of his fingernail and began to bleed. "I'll be mixing you in with our regular infantry, there won't be room for you to set up separately." The captain wiped the ear blood with his forefinger and smudged it onto his blue wool pants.

"Ya give me a wall for cover I'll do real fine, sir, just happy to be back with the infantry...those horse boys make me plenty nervous."

"Excellent, Wells, now fall in there behind the last man, it's only a little over a mile to where we're going." The captain walked off and the column of troops started to move forward.

Wells pulled the green kepi down tight on his head and followed the 11th Pennsylvania into the woods, north toward Oak Ridge.

The temperature spiked higher, hot enough to sharpen the air with the scent of sap oozing down the pine trunks. Acrid smoke, mixed with the smell of burned flesh, wafted through the foliage. Wells tried to ignore it, wanted to get his mind onto better things. He started to sweat. The jumpy motion of the march pushed up his heartbeat. A rough patch of skin on the back of his legs itched where it rubbed against his wool pants.

His thoughts wandered back to a cold winter afternoon five years before. It was the last time he had been so uncomfortable in his clothes. On a Thanksgiving Wednesday he had taken Thomas on a turkey hunting expedition in the woods west of Waterloo along the Seneca-Cayuga Canal. He wanted to show Thomas the ways of the woods. Wildlife often came down to the canal in late afternoon to drink, so he took his brother to a favorite spot where they could climb to a perch in an oak tree by the water. As he pulled himself up his foot slipped on an icy branch and he fell into the canal. It wasn't deep, but he felt foolish.

His brother knew the dangers of standing dripping wet on a frigid November evening. James started to shiver and shake. His clothes clung to his body like icy boards. Thomas took James's stiff jacket and shirt off, replaced it with his own, then started a fire and held his brother. James never forgot it.

Walking through the hot Pennsylvania woods, Wells kept the good thoughts of his brother close and prayed he would never see him in a Confederate uniform. After a quarter hour of marching, mostly under the cover of dense woods, the 11th Pennsylvania approached an opening. The first sergeant waved them to crouch low as they prepared to cross a mown meadow leading to a rough stone wall, a farmer's wall about half the height of a man.

"Single file, move it, keep your damn heads down," growled the first sergeant.

Wells crawled the last few yards through the rough scrabble, propped his gun against the wall and turned to see the last man clear the woods. He looked up and down the wall. The stooped run from the woods exhausted him. Everyone sat out of breath, their backs pressed to the wall. Wells closed his eyes and pretended he was somewhere else. He scratched his leg and felt a rash forming on his calf. *Time to rip off this damn uniform,* he thought, *and jump naked into the cold water of Seneca Lake back home.*

The still air sucked his breath away. He rolled over onto his knees for a look through a chink in the wall. The stone blocks felt like a half-heated oven. Pine trees shimmered in the distance beyond a clover field that rose gently to the right. Except for the wall, there was no cover anywhere. It was much too quiet.

Two things turned in his mind: his field of fire was clear, that was good, but the regiment's field position could not have been worse. Little had changed since the morning. The Union line remained thin and extended, and worst of all, the Yanks were outnumbered. If the Rebs hit directly into their right flank they would easily roll up the men waiting behind the wall and collapse the entire Union line. Quick retreat would be the only option.

Wells looked back to gauge the best path to safety. The woods were about fifty yards from the wall. There was no chance he'd make it there, better to run down the ridge along the wall.

"Here they come!"

He raised his eye to the hole and looked up to the right where flags appeared just past the top of the hill, a mile away.

A sergeant crawled up from behind and put his hand on Wells' shoulder. "Private, take a look through your scope, what regiments do ya make out?" The sergeant looked old beyond his years. Half his teeth were broken and all were stained orange from chewing tobacco. Jagged scar tissue ran diagonally across his left cheek. "There, Private, up there, what ya see?" The sergeant's breath smelled of coffee and garlic. Wells turned away, then lifted his rifle into the hole and pressed his eye to the lens.

"My God, Sergeant, there's a bunch of brigades coming up."

"Can ya make out any regimental flags? Look to the right."

He moved his rifle smoothly toward the north end of the hill and focused in on a group of Rebs forming there. The superheated atmosphere distorted the distant view, and at first he could not make out the regimental numbers. "Wait...it's Carolina, sir, but I'm not sure..." He tried to steady the scope to compensate for the jumpy air. "It's an N...

yes...got it...it's North...North Carolina...there's at least five flags but I can only make out three...the 5th, 23rd and 12th."

The sergeant knelt to speak with the men. "It's Rode's division just as we expected, he's loaded with Carolina boys, Iverson's Brigade for sure." He pointed down the wall toward Gettysburg, then squinted into the sun. "We've only got two regiments on the wall..." He paused, looked down for a moment, then looked up into his men's eyes. "We're all that's holding back those Southern boys from sweeping the Union right back through town. God knows, the best we can do is delay them...slow down the Secesh until our main corps comes up tonight."

"What's your plan for me, Sergeant?" Wells began, "I got 'em in my range now."

"No one fires yet! The first Reb sees us behind this wall we're finished. Keep low, make no sound, and pray men...pray they don't see us until they're here, it's our only chance." He crossed himself and kissed his ring. "No one fires 'til I raise my arm."

Just then a dog came running out of the woods, eyes bulging, saliva flying. The dog, a bull terrier, burst into the middle of the men and pawed the sergeant. "Hey, doggie, best git your ass down, the Rebs be coming." Everyone in the regiment knew this dog had two things she could not abide, women and Confederates.

"Corporal, ya keep dis pooch here quiet 'til the shooting begins then turn her loose on those bastards! Ya hear that, doggie...ya follow orders now?" The sergeant turned and crawled down the line to talk to the next company. His garlic scent hung in the air.

Wells knew the 5th Carolina. His brother's regiment was on the left end of the line, the end that would reach the wall first. Wells expected to die. The section of the Union line where he sat faced at least a five-to-one Confederate advantage. "Maybe it's for the best," he whispered, "I'll be dead before Thomas shows up."

Iverson's brigade continued to form on the crest of the hill. Wells watched through his scope, and picked out who to target when his chance came. It seemed strange how long the Rebs were taking to get organized. He could not have known that General Iverson was off his game that day. Iverson had taken a measure of the ground before him and miscalculated where the Union line began. He paid no attention to the wall that concealed the Union troops, in fact, he didn't move off the line with his men. Iverson, a privileged Southerner, the son of a Georgia senator and only a little over 30 years old, remained at the top of the hill. His troops needed his guidance but instead he sent out inexperienced junior officers to lead the advance.

Wells saw the North Carolina men coming with no skirmishers out front, no one to check out what lay ahead. It was a grievous mistake. At first the Rebel regiments moved away, but then they started to drift to their left in a direction that would carry them near the wall, right in front of the Union guns.

"They have no idea we're here." Wells poked the corporal. "We'll be shooting right into their flank as they pass!" The corporal shook his head, incredulous but pleased. Everyone kept quiet, it was all too good to be true. The men could now hear the rustle of the Rebel troops stepping through the grass, the tinkling of metal against metal on their belts. A soft breeze washed over the hill and brought the smell of the Rebs to the wall, a pungent mix of old tobacco, unwashed bodies and wood smoke. All eyes focused on the sergeant.

Wells took another look through his scope, but the Carolina men were too close to see in focus. The corporal nudged Wells. "They're here, right opposite us."

The sergeant's hand went up. Down the line came the faint sounds of men clenching their rifles, moving up to a low crouch, then leaning into the wall and taking aim. A tremendous volley shook the ground. There was no need to aim, all the Yankees had to do was point toward the mass of Iverson's men.

The shock of the simultaneous blasts stung Wells's ears and raised a cloud of dust that mixed into the black powder smoke from the guns. The dense blinding whirlwind washed through openings in the wall. The rebels screamed, but not the Rebel yell, it was a hellish cry of shock, pain and death. The men of the 11th Pennsylvania kept shooting into the blinding miasma.

"Hold your fire!" screamed the sergeant. Everyone reloaded and waited, desperate for a view of the Carolinians.

Wells dropped down and looked through a low opening where the air was clearer. What was left of Iverson's brigade lay exactly as they had marched, hundreds of men down, all in perfect order, their feet resting in straight lines. The living crawled toward a slight depression in the field, but it afforded little protection.

The smoke cleared and the Yanks started firing into the men pressed to the ground. There was no place to hide. The Rebs tried to raise white rags, some even took off their socks and waved them. A smaller group to the right had deeper cover and began to form a charge from their position opposite Wells.

"Watch yourselves," warned the sergeant, "look to the front."

Most of the Pennsylvanians concentrated on shooting the exposed men trapped to the left and missed the other group. Wells had seen it all and was ready for the charge. He picked off the first Reb who approached his section, then, just to his left, he saw a platoon led by an officer.

"Oh, my God!" Wells reached out and grabbed the corporal's arm.

"What is it?" The corporal didn't understand, he saw nothing to warrant Wells' alarm. There were just ten Rebs who would never make it to the wall.

"It's Thomas!"

"Thomas! What are you talking about?"

"My brother! The Confederate captain...he's my brother!"

The rest happened very quickly. Before the corporal could react Wells jumped over the wall and ran toward the Rebels. Thomas recognized his brother when they had closed to thirty yards.

"Go back, Thomas!" screamed Wells. Everyone stopped, frozen in their tracks. The Union corporal signaled for his company to hold their fire to avoid hitting James, but that was asking a lot, especially with Wells wearing the green sharpshooters coat. "Run Thomas!" he yelled, but the Rebels held their ground. Thomas' eyes bulged, raw with fear.

One of the Rebs asked Thomas what was happening. "It's my brother, the Yank's my brother."

James raised his Whitworth and aimed it toward his brother to move him back. "Go, Captain, now!" It was this action which everyone saw so differently: the Rebels saw it as an attack; Thomas knew his brother was trying to save him; the Yankees behind the wall took it as a signal to resume firing.

"Damn you, James," shouted Thomas. He reached for his revolver, but before he could raise it, James fired in a last desperate attempt to move the Rebs back. His aim was perfect, the shot whizzed past Thomas' ear, close enough to frighten him, but there was another perfect shot. At exactly the moment that James pulled the trigger a round came from behind, from the wall and caught Thomas in the throat, ripping out the back of his neck.

"Son a bitch Yanks!" screamed one of the Rebs. "His brother shot the captain." With that they all turned to fire at James, who remained standing a few yards from his fallen brother. Another heavy volley from the Union side cut through the air. James fell to the ground, sure he had been hit, afraid to move. He opened one eye and looked for the Rebs, but they were gone. Two had been wounded, the rest ran for cover.

"Private Wells!" screamed the sergeant. "Git your ass back here!" James looked down for a moment then turned toward his brother's body.

"Wells!" came the voice again. A Rebel shot ricocheted off the dirt by Wells's hand, scattering shards into his eye. He snatched his rifle and raced for the wall.

Coda

Iverson's Brigade lost nearly a thousand men that afternoon, most in a few terrible seconds. General Iverson was removed from command for the rest of the battle and is forever remembered for his blunderous leadership on July 1. Not long after Wells made it back to the wall, all Union forces began to pull back in the face of overwhelming waves of Rebels arriving on the field. Nevertheless, the stubborn Yankee resistance slowed Lee's army enough to prevent him from taking the high ground to the east before nightfall. The Rebels chased the smaller Union force through Gettysburg toward Cemetery Ridge, but by then it was too late. Union troops had come up and secured the high ground, setting up the battlefield advantage that, over the next two tragic days, would favor the Union.

That night, the fields where Iverson's Regiments had been cut down were well behind Confederate lines. Lee's men, working by torch light, came onto the slopes along Oak Ridge and buried the dead of the North Carolina regiments in shallow trenches. Over the years this area of intensely concentrated graves came to be known as Iverson's Pits. The Gettysburg farmers never lost track of where it was, the crops thrived there. Whether it was the spectral lights that spontaneously ignited above the trenches in the months after the battle or the superstitious nature of the locals, to this day most are uncomfortable going near Iverson's Pits after dark. It is exactly there that Captain Thomas Wells still lies.

Part Two

SAVAGES STATION

Knowledge is ultimately self-knowledge
and self-knowledge is the soul seen by itself.
CICERO

PRELUDE

The general's left arm was a mess. The first minnie ball shattered his humerus bone, another nicked his ulna. A third projectile cut through his hand, shattering the carpal bones. The damage could not be repaired; amputation was the only hope.

Chloroform would spare the soldier most of the pain but it would do nothing for the weary surgeon. The doctor had never operated on a friend and for the first time since the war began he tasted fear.

The surgeon wiped the brow of his comrade and motioned the assistant to pour the anesthetic. Then, before he lost his nerve, the doctor reached for a long curved knife, still bloody and soiled from hours of work. No water remained to wash the instruments, much less the hands of the surgeon. The tent was hot and the little water available was needed to slake the thirst of the wounded. Sweat glistened on the bare chests and bloody arms of the surgical team.

It ended in a flash of the knife and a few vigorous saw strokes. A sergeant moved to catch the arm and carry it to the pile of limbs stacked behind the tent, but a chaplain blocked the way. He held out a clean wool blanket and motioned the sergeant to drop it into the folds. The chaplain wrapped it quickly, nodded and disappeared into the night.

THE ARCHIVES

The words on the ancient paper made no sense.

...Fabrizio besought his comrades not to leave him there to fall into Rebel hands, but circumstances compelled us to leave him...

Elizabeth had spent three weeks combing through Civil War records, bits and pieces of information that detailed the mayhem and tragic losses served up to countless men and women in uniform between 1861 and 1865. Perhaps countless wasn't accurate, but it seemed that way to her. After dwelling for days among the dusty records of the fallen, she knew better than most how many had died. It was the loss of 620,000 lives in the American Civil War that a new memorial in Waterloo, New York, was to commemorate. Elizabeth, the descendant of a Civil War artillery officer, had come to the National Archives in Washington to do research for the memorial project, to review the files of the fifty-eight fallen of Waterloo.

"Excuse me, Elizabeth, here are the rest of the files," said the clerk. "We will be closing in an hour, please place them in the cart when you leave." The archives employee was a small, energetic woman. If it had not been for her, Elizabeth would never have found Corporal Fabrizio Cenci's file.

"Look at this," said Elizabeth, holding a frayed yellow paper up for the clerk to see. It was a letter fragment from a soldier in the 33rd New York Regiment, written years after the war ended. She found it in a blue linen envelope clipped to Fabrizio's Military Service Record. The brown ink had darkened almost to black but the cursive was well formed and easy to read.

"What is it?" The clerk took a quick look but saw nothing unusual.

"Here..." Elizabeth put the paper flat on the oak table and pointed to a sentence. "Here, look, I can't believe what it says."

"What's upsetting you, dear?" The clerk wasn't sure how seriously to take her. Elizabeth was an adolescent, a junior in high school. She had spent weeks combing through aging letters and documents written in ink, letters full of the pain of desperate widows trying to feed their children, and anxious to find their missing sons and husbands. The brittle texture of the papers had invaded her dreams.

"I'm not upset," she lied, "just read it..." The clerk put her hand on Elizabeth's shoulder, tried to settle her down, and wondered if the war files were too much for an eager young student. Elizabeth, with her blond bobbed hair and matching turquoise pants and sweater, was the picture of innocence. She twirled a yellow pencil through her fingers like a cheerleader's baton and slid the document toward the clerk.

"They deserted him! He was a wounded man, and they left him for the Rebs," she said, her hazel eyes wide open. "They just up and left him to die...I have never seen anything like this in hundreds of records."

"Cenci...he's a Waterloo man I suspect?"

"Yes, one of the fifty-eight fallen. He was only seventeen when he enlisted, barely eighteen when he went missing at Savages Station." Elizabeth looked up at the clerk. She expected a little understanding. Elizabeth had been struck by the young age of the soldiers. It had become personal for her—many of the dead were her own age.

The clerk had worked at the National Archives for twenty-eight years. Nothing much surprised her anymore. "I know it's hard to imagine, men were left behind..."

"But the wounded, the sick, left to be abused, slaughtered by the enemy?" Elizabeth looked again for a response but the clerk froze as if something were wrong. Elizabeth could not have known, but the clerk was from tidewater Virginia and was not pleased with the way she spoke of Southerners as the abusive enemy. Negative talk about Southerners always irritated her.

"Look here," said the clerk, pointing to two new files in the cart. "There's additional documents on your Corporal Fabrizio...maybe you'll find out what happened." With that she turned and walked away.

Elizabeth watched as she crossed the room, winding her way between long tables set with green-shaded lamps. The late-afternoon sun poured through high clerestory windows and bathed the desks in golden light. Only one other researcher sat in the great space. The clerk dropped a file on his desk and left the room.

"So that was that," said Elizabeth. "My corporal has been abandoned to the enemy and the clerk doesn't want to talk about it." She stood and reached for the new files. The first was a thin blue folder marked Corporal Fabrizio Cenci, Pension File. Next to it was a thick green accordion envelope with the words Thomas Jonathan Jackson scratched in black ink on the flap. She looked around to see if anyone was looking. Archive rules prohibited the removal of more than one file at a time from the cart. Just then the clerk came up the stairs so Elizabeth left both files and sat back down.

"Rules, rules..." she whispered. To amuse herself while she waited for the clerk to disappear, she flipped through the much too adult *Archive Handout* listing *Do's and Don'ts for Researchers*: *Visitors are prohibited from bringing in a purse, briefcase, notebook, highlighters, pens, hat or coat. Also prohibited are sweaters with zippers, drinking water, envelopes and folders.* These were rules that would irritate most adults, but for an adolescent they were intolerable. Fortunately, the rules permitted a laptop and she quickly learned how to use it to get around most of the don'ts. There she kept copies of her notes and a PDF index of The Waterloo Military Record Book 1861-1865. She flipped open her MacBook Pro, double clicked on the PDF icon, then scrolled to the handwritten entry on Fabrizio Cenci:

> *Corporal, 33rd Regiment, Co C: Born Waterloo 1844 ~ laborer and native of Waterloo ~ single, 5'9" tall, sandy complexion, hazel eyes, black hair ~ Enlisted July 26, 1861 ~ Mustered August, 1861 ~ Single ~ $2 Relief granted to family by Town ~ Supposed to be dead, last seen at Savages Station before arrival of Jackson Brigade*

The mention of the Jackson Brigade caught her eye. There were no other leads to Fabrizio's disappearance, so she had asked the clerk to pull the file of Thomas Jonathan Jackson, hoping there might be some clue in the Rebel commander's file. It was a long shot, but maybe she'd learn what General Jackson found in Savages Station.

Corporal Cenci's file was thick and the details of his time in the war broke her heart. He had been abandoned by his comrades in the steaming chaos of the Peninsula Campaign. But why he was left remained elusive. Elizabeth was no soldier, but she knew the last thing an infantryman would do is hand a comrade to the enemy, especially a sick or wounded friend. And yet, that is what had happened; the records she had reviewed were clear on this. And so it was with great anticipation that she opened Corporal Cenci's Pension File and held up the first page, titled "Claim for Mother's Pension."

"Keep that page flat on the table, young lady, please!"

"Oh my God, you startled me!"

"Sorry, Elizabeth…you know better."

"…it's just that…I didn't see you…your voice…I'm sorry."

"Keep your papers flat on the table, dear. We don't want any damage now do we?"

OK, thought Elizabeth, *control yourself, the "school monitor" will be gone in a moment. Don't do anything stupid and get thrown out.*

She looked up and cracked her best Shirley Temple smile, then put the paper down. "Yes, yes, it won't happen again."

"Oh, I forgot to tell you, there's something quite unusual in the Thomas Jonathan Jackson file."

"What would that be?"

"Here, look," she said, pointing to a red label on the outside of the file with the word Firenze scratched on the paper. "There's a folder inside with letters and notes about Jackson's trip to Italy before the war. Not many people know he was a tourist before he was a famous general." Elizabeth took the file and brushed the dust off the red label with her forefinger. "Oh, one more thing, dear, I found a Waterloo file on a slave, a Sergeant Jeremiah something…looks interesting. He met up with Harriet Tubman on the run from Vicksburg." The clerk hesitated a moment, then turned and disappeared into the ladies room.

"Please, just stay away," whispered Elizabeth, "go bother someone else." She looked around to see if any other clerks were lurking in the background then turned her attention back to Corporal Cenci.

Cenci's Pension File began with the claim form submitted by Fabrizio's mother on October 7, 1865. In it she attested to her son's enlistment, conjectured death, and the support he had provided her while in the army. There were pages of letters, affidavits, and certifications supporting her claim but only two documents that revealed any new information on the disappearance of Fabrizio. The first was a letter fragment from the commander of Company C and the second was a deposition from a sergeant in the same company. Captain Chester Cold wrote the following in neat black script:

> *...for several weeks Cenci had been suffering from Diarrhea, - he often fell out unable to keep up with the Regiment. - the last that I saw him was a day or two before the Battle of Savages Station...I was soon afterwards informed Cenci was taken prisoner or died at Savages Station.*

Elizabeth knew Fabrizio was not well when he went missing but she had assumed he was wounded, not sick. In fact, both the Union and Confederate armies were riddled with disease. More soldiers succumbed to sickness than died in combat. The soldiers fighting in the area around Savages Station endured severe conditions. The weather was oppressively hot and the terrain was lousy with swamps, creeks, biting insects, and a fair number of poisonous reptiles. Elizabeth placed Captain Cold's letter back in the file and brought out the deposition from Sergeant Eric Brown.

> *State of New York Seneca County: Eric Brown being duly sworn says that he was a member of Co. C. 33 Regiment N. Y. Volunteers during the Campaign of the Federal Forces on the Peninsula in Virginia in 1862 and knew Fabrizio Cenci who was suffering severely from chronic diarrhea. That when deponent saw him at Savages Station, he was so feeble that he was able to speak only in whispers & was exhausted in strength, so as to be unable to help himself, and was apparently near death; deponent thought he could survive but a few hours. About this time the Federal forces were leaving Savages Station, and said Fabrizio begged his Comrades not to abandon him, but circumstances compelled them to leave him.*

>| | | |
>|--------------|---|--------|
>| *23rd day* |) | *his* |
>| *of June* |) | *Eric* ✗ *Brown* |
>| *1864* |) | *mark* |

Over the past weeks Elizabeth had become attached to Fabrizio and felt angry when she read the Brown depositon. There was no doubt—Fabrizio had been deserted by his comrades to face the enemy alone and helpless. She tried to imagine how he must have felt. She couldn't understand how he could have been left to die.

No other information existed in any of Fabrizio's files, nothing to shed light on the moment when the enemy arrived, what he endured, what became of him. Eager to learn more, she reached to open the Jackson file, but in the process of closing Fabrizio's papers a tear fell near the X at the bottom of Sergeant Brown's deposition. She moved to wipe it away, then thought better of it and let it soak into the paper.

Basilica di Santo Croce

Thomas Jonathan Jackson pulled hard on the ancient bronze handle and looked through the portal into the great church. Cool air flowed out of the interior, soothing his scorched face. The day had been hot, hotter even than the dog days of August in Virginia, and he prayed that maybe here was a cool place in sweltering Florence.

Fifty years earlier Napoleon had complained about the heat of Italy, but Thomas hadn't expected it would be this bad. Lately, his mind dwelled on the great French warrior. He had recently visited Belgium to see the battlefield at Waterloo, and had passed through Switzerland across the Alps into Italy. He had purposely taken the Simplon Pass, the same route Napoleon followed when he invaded Italy. Jackson, a mathematics and artillery instructor at Virginia Military Institute, knew a great deal about Napoleon, but not nearly enough about Tuscan weather.

His hand still on the door, he turned to look back into the piazza at the rough gray pavement stones baking in the noon heat. Off to his left, storm clouds hung in the eastern sky offering hope of relief. Sharp, hot gusts blew dust and bits of pigeon feathers across his face. *Now,* he thought, *now is the time to cross the threshold, this is the place you've waited so long to see.*

The massive bronze door closed with a sharp *click.* Fragrant air drew him forward, away from the inferno of mid-August in the Mediterranean world. The masonry walls, the marble floor, and the stone sculptures held enough of the winter cold to keep the interior cool. He had read much about the church, even studied engravings of the interior. Santa Croce was the highlight of his extended European tour of England, France, Belgium, Germany and Switzerland. Soon he would return to Virginia, and he knew life would never be the same again. He had viewed hundreds of master paintings and sculptures, but his greatest pleasure came from walking through the mysterious spaces of ancient buildings, especially the churches. A year later he would pen this in his notebook:

Passing over the works of the Creator, which are far the most impressive, it is difficult to conceive of the influence which even the works of His creatures exercise over the mind till one loiters amidst their master productions. Well do I remember the influence of sculpture upon me during my short stay in Florence...

The space was huge. Frescoed chapels beckoned in the distance, earthen colors of sienna and mauve mixed with the glow of turquoise and gold leaf. He turned to the right to light a candle and to pray. Jackson, a deeply religious man, thought back to October, nearly two years before, when he lost his wife, Ellie, and their stillborn son. His world had frozen; there seemed no clear way forward. For twenty months he had mourned, his friends hardly recognized him. Then, one day he looked up and said he was leaving for Europe.

New York City, July 1856

My Dear Sister:

I sail in the steamship Asia *for Europe at twelve today for Liverpool...you are a very kind and affectionate sister, yet even with you I would be reminded of the loss of happiness which I once enjoyed with dear Ellie. So I have to some extent torn myself away from that state of mind which I feared, should my summer have been passed at home...I hope you will be able to get up the tombstones by the aid of the money I have sent you...*

The sudden trip to Europe made no sense to anyone but Thomas. He was a soldier, a military professor, assuredly not a man of culture. His students considered him eccentric, sometimes difficult, and his personal losses had only accentuated these problems. Months of ennui in Virginia had convinced him that he must move on or forever weep, so he sailed to the old world to immerse himself in the arts, to seek the wisdom, the mystery of the masters, and to find new direction.

He looked down at the candles in the bronze rack, picked one up and turned the soft tallow taper in his hand. *Ellie would have liked this,* he thought. They were devoutly Protestant, not comfortable lighting candles in churches, but the Catholic traditions made sense here and helped shift his mind to new ways of seeing. He leaned forward, touched the wick to a flame, held the fragrant candle up to his face, close enough to feel the heat, close enough to feel the presence of Ellie.

"Here, signore, this is what you've come to see." Thomas turned toward the voice. Enrico, his guide in Florence, put his hand on Jackson's back and directed him toward the right wall of the church.

"It's the tomb of Michelangelo Buonaroti," said Enrico in a reverent, hushed voice. Enrico, a portly olive-complexioned man with swept-back red hair full of comb marks, pointed ahead. Piercing gray eyes, a long scar on his left cheek, and an angular Roman nose gave him the look of an ancient emperor, perhaps a Maxentius or even a Valentinian. But he was no emperor, just a common foot soldier. When he was a young man, Enrico had fought with assorted armies and mercenary bands in the endless, confusing Italian wars. Sometimes city fought city, but more often a foreign army provided the opposition. He had tried to make it to Milan when Napoleon invaded but had been too late. Now he earned his living as a guide in Florence and told war stories to his amused travelers.

"Here, stand here," whispered Enrico, "so you can see while I talk." When Enrico had first met Jackson he assumed he was just another American on the grand tour looking to see a few sights and drink some Chianti. Jackson's appearance was not distinctive. He was rather plain with a sharply receding hairline, broad face, and full beard. The Italian sun had not been kind to his fair complexion. He looked much better in profile. A finely chiseled nose and wavy brown hair gave him the look of the face of Gregory XVI on the Vatican five-scudi gold piece.

It was when he first spoke that Enrico knew there was more to the man than his appearance. "I'd be mighty obliged," he said, "if you'd show me what the Italians love most about your city, not what you reckon an American might be interested in." And so Enrico was released from his normal responsibilities. He enjoyed parts of what he did but he hated taking tourists over and over again to the same places.

Enrico showed Jackson things very few visitors had ever seen. They went to see the Last Supper at Sant' Apollonia, they saw the Crucifixion by Perugino at Santa Maria Maddalena De' Pazzi, and all the Fra Angelico frescoes at San Marco. Jackson was particularly interested in the Annunciation at the top of San Marco's stairs, the way the angel Gabriel knelt, and the look in Mary's eyes. Perhaps most memorable was the visit to the Medici Chapel at San Lorenzo. There, in the Cappella dei Principi, Enrico pointed out the many reliquaries with fingers, jaw bones, and arms of the saints.

"You Italians collect mighty unusual objects."

"But this is nothing," Enrico replied, pointing to a shelf of finger bones. "When the chapel was built, plans were laid to steal the Holy Sepulchre from Jerusalem and place it where you now stand, but instead we have this, a few sacred bones."

At first, Thomas had been secretive about his personal life but as Enrico surprised him again and again with little-known sights he started to open up, to speak about why he had come. The greatest surprise came when Enrico told him about the day he saw Napoleon. Jackson in turn revealed he was also a soldier, a veteran of the Mexican War. From that moment a strong friendship developed.

One thing about Thomas set him apart from anyone Enrico had ever met—he always had a lemon in his pocket. On the second day, when they were walking in the Boboli Gardens, Jackson spotted a lemon tree, snatched a piece of the sour fruit and ate it like an apple. Jackson's eccentricities appealed to Enrico.

Near the end of Jackson's visit Enrico took him on one of his favorite strolls, up the Via di San Leonardo past Galileo's house to the little Church of San Leonardo. On the way back they stopped at the Forte Belvedere for the view over the city. It was near sunset and cool breezes washed up the cypress-covered hills. Enrico reached in his pocket and took out two biscotti wrapped in parchment paper. Thomas tried to chew off a piece.

"Reckon this is as hard as an old book cover. Reminds me of what we used to carry in our pockets in Mexico."

Enrico laughed. "No, no, it's too hard like that." He took out a small bottle of white wine and poured some on the biscotti. "Now taste it."

The flavor and texture were transformed. The cookie melted in his mouth, hints of almond, vanilla, and spice coated his tongue. Jackson felt so good he decided to surprise his friend.

"Signor Enrico, tomorrow is our last day together. You must take me to see Michelangelo's tomb, I'd be deeply appreciative." And so, the next day, they made their way to Santa Croce.

"The building is more than I anticipated," said Jackson, gesturing toward Santa Croce's main altar.

"Forgive me, Thomas, but there is pain in your eyes."

"This place brings me joy but it is mixed with sadness." He put his hands to his face, thumbs under his chin, his forefingers resting on his nose as if he were praying. "The perfection here, the wondrous works by so many masters reminds me how incomplete my life is, how much I have lost."

"I'm sorry, my friend." He too had recently lost his wife but had not told Thomas. "Look up, look into the eyes of Michelangelo... " He pointed to the bust of the master resting atop the sarcophagus. "Never fear the incomplete, my friend. Michelangelo left most of his sculptures unfinished...don't you think it makes them more interesting? Perhaps it's why we love them."

Jackson reached out to feel the cool marble. The monument, engaged into the wall of the church, rose nearly four times his height. In the middle, six feet off the floor, Michelangelo's stone sarcophagus rested behind three seated marble figures.

"The three female figures represent..." began Enrico, but Thomas motioned him to stop.

"I came to stand in Michelangelo's presence, not to admire the art carved on his tomb," Thomas said, then placed his left hand on the guide's arm. "Enrico, I was a young soldier when I first learned of Michelangelo; my staff sergeant whose father was born in Rome spoke often of the great artist's work, especially the *David*. The sergeant died in the Battle of Molino del Rey, cut down by a shot to the heart. He wanted me to see the master's work, to pray at his tomb."

"Your sergeant was a wise man, every student in Italy learns of Michelangelo at a young age."

Jackson wasn't listening. He pulled his hand back and lowered his head.

"What is greatness, Enrico? Is it the power we gain over others, or is it the beauty of our creations?"

Enrico shook his head. "Michelangelo would have known."

"You showed me his Pieta in the Duomo. He included himself in the sculpture, in the person of Nicodemus holding up the body of Christ...Michelangelo was a devout man, wasn't he?"

Enrico turned toward the muffled sound of a brown-robed monk shuffling across the transept with a paintbrush in his hand. Outside, from beyond the Arno, across the distant hills, the first faint rumble of thunder worked its way over the city walls, through the streets and into the great nave. Jackson looked up. Sunlight sent oblique shafts of colored light across the terra cotta floor. His thoughts turned back to his wife.

"I fell in love when I was nearly thirty, and in a year it was all gone..." He looked into Enrico's eyes. "Tell me, was Michelangelo in love?"

"Some say as much, but I think mostly he was in love with his Carrara marble."

"His work affects me in ways I cannot explain – you've been good to show it to me." Jackson paused for a moment, then crossed back into the nave. His eye wandered up to the polychromed wood ceiling, then down the long catwalks strung below the clerestory windows. In his mind he was rewriting a letter he had sent to his aunt a year earlier. He intended to compose similar letters to his friends before he left for Europe, but dared not.

...your kind letter, so full of sympathy and love made a deep impression on my stricken heart. I can hardly realize yet that my dear Ellie is no more...that she will never again welcome my return...no more soothe my troubled spirit by her ever kind, sympathizing heart, words and love...

In the distance, a sacristan lit the candles on the high altar, the smoke from the match lingering in the air, turned blue by the light of the stained glass.

"How old is this place? Much older than Virginia I'm sure?"

Enrico smiled. "Much older, my friend, so old no one knows for sure, but most historians use the date 1295. That's a few years before our Cristofo Columbo came to America, no?"

Jackson looked away, his eyes following the sacristan as he fumbled in his coat for a key, opened a carved wood door, and disappeared. "I can feel time here, it's in the light, the smell of the candles, the incense."

"Signore, there is something I want to show you, maybe it will be of help." Enrico took Thomas by the arm and started to move him toward the side aisle but Jackson resisted.

"Forgive me, Enrico, I must do something." He walked back to Michelangelo's tomb, and stood in front of the middle marble figure, a mourning woman with her head tilted onto her upraised right hand. He stepped up onto the monument's pietra serena base, then reached out and checked the depth of a long vertical marble fold along her left calf.

"It's perfect," whispered Thomas. "No one will know." He opened his hand to reveal two small stones.

"What are those, signore?"

"I've brought them across the ocean...stones from the tombs of Elizabeth and Ellie." He reached out and dropped one into the bottom of a deep crevice next to the woman's right foot. "I was two years old when my sister Elizabeth died in Clarksburg in 1826. She was six... typhoid fever broke her."

"You were so young..."

"It's the only thing I remember of my earliest years...death seems to hold our memory, doesn't it?" He dropped a second stone into another crevice, then knelt on the floor with his face and open hands pressed against the tomb wall. The eternal cool of the white marble chilled his forehead. He tried to imagine how Michelangelo must have felt when he viewed the completed Pieta with his own face on the figure of Nicodemus. He closed his eyes and saw his sister, still six years old.

"No one will know, signore. Your stones are safe, it's a good thing."

Jackson stood and rubbed his face. "Now, my dear Enrico, show me what you wish."

The tempest outside drew nearer, the sky light wavered, then went dark. Enrico crossed himself, kissed his right hand, then took Jackson by the arm and moved him to the left, toward the next tomb.

"Maybe now I will be your Virgil," said Enrico, a big smile on his face. "Today we finish our journey."

Three candles burned on the mensa in front of them. "Tell me, what tomb is this?"

He pointed to two words incised in the base just below the sarcophagus: *Dante Aligherio*. "It's the Latin spelling, but you recognize the first name, no, signore?"

Thomas knew. "This is Dante, but I can hardly believe my eyes."

"You see," whispered Enrico, "our great artists are not always painters and sculptors."

"I read the *Inferno* at West Point, it didn't have much in common with what we learned there..." He paused, thought for a moment. "Or maybe it did."

Thomas looked slowly up and down the tomb. The monument had three marble figures, two women, one collapsed in grief on the end of the sarcophagus and Dante sitting above in a pensive pose. The scale of the figures was much larger than Michelangelo's tomb, almost double life-size. There were laurel leaves everywhere, symbols of Dante's exalted position in the poetic firmament. Enrico stared at Thomas, a slight grin breaking the line of his mouth.

"What, Enrico? Speak to me."

"It's not a tomb."

"But there is a sarcophagus?"

"It's empty."

"Empty, someone stole the body?"

"They tried."

"Who tried?"

"It's a cenotaph, Dante was never here, he fled for his life as a young man...never returned to Florence."

"Why, why did he flee?"

"He was an innocent on the wrong side of Florentine politics, the times were dangerous." Enrico drew a flattened hand across his throat. "He lost everything, his home, his loved ones." A bright flash of light illuminated their faces as thunder reverberated through the nave. "He was like you, Thomas, life as he knew it ripped away at a young age, he had to reinvent himself."

Jackson gazed up into Dante's marble face. "Why is this monument here if they ran him out?"

"He willed himself into a new life, created beauty, became the world's most famous poet."

"He didn't return?"

"Florence invited him back."

"And..."

"He refused, he never returned, so they built this. You can't steal beauty but they tried. Many people think he's here."

"Where is he?"

"In Ravenna. He spent his last years there. The Florentines went to Ravenna in the middle of the night to abduct his body but it was too well hidden, so the sarcophagus in front of you remains empty."

Jackson looked away, couldn't imagine such things. "You're telling me the great city of Florence robs graves?"

"Yes, my friend. In Italy we fight over many things, but especially the bodies of the famous, the holy. When Michelangelo died in Rome, we snuck his body out in a hay wagon and here he rests. Perugia and Assisi fought for years over the body of Saint Francis. Many of the bones you saw in the Medici Chapel were – well what is the best way to say this – acquired in secret ways. Did you know that the body of San Marco now rests in Venice because the Doge sent a ship to Alexandria to steal the corpse?"

Thomas looked at Enrico with a blank expression, tried to understand.

"Every tomb has a story, look behind you, across the nave." The far wall was lined with more altars and tombs. "There." Enrico motioned with his right arm raised. "Look, the last one on the left, near the doors."

Jackson started to walk across the nave. Enrico suppressed a laugh, he couldn't believe Jackson's erect military gait. He grabbed at his arm to slow him down. "Perhaps it's better if I first begin the story from a distance." Thomas nodded, happy to stay where he was.

"A great Tuscan lies in this tomb, another man who had to reinvent himself. He was persecuted and nearly executed for the truth of his

58

work. Unlike Dante he did not create new worlds, rather he found them, places only he had the genius to reveal."

"But who is it?"

"Go...see for yourself."

Jackson crossed the nave. He could not find a name amongst all the Latin phrases incised into the tomb's marble surfaces.

"Here, give me your hand." Enrico took Jackson's forefinger and brushed it over two words, *Galileo Galilei*.

"I know you are a man of precision, of mathematics, so I'm sure I need not recount his story."

Thomas looked stunned. "This man is one of my heroes..."

"Yes, he is here, your hand rests on his tomb." Jackson backed away to see it better, and Enrico continued. "But there are parts of his story you may not know. His daughter, his oldest child, remained closest to his heart. She spent her life doing good works in a convent on the hill just across the Arno from here. She died in 1634 after a bout of dysentery. She was thirty-four, her father seventy. He withdrew into months of desperate mourning, his health declined, his heart began to skip beats, he had palpitations."

Jackson squinted, rubbed his beard. "Tell me, what was her name?"

"Virginia, a word dear to your own heart I'm sure."

Jackson's mouth started to form the first semblance of a smile but then disappeared.

Enrico motioned toward the tomb. "Galileo was a religious man... like yourself. He read spiritual writings to console himself. In his grief he often heard Virginia calling out to him...he had visions."

Jackson turned in the direction of another flash of lightning, the thunder now much diminished.

"Galileo lived eight years after Virginia's burial. In 1637, five years before his death, he went blind. Pope Urban VIII hounded Galileo, preventing him from being interred here in the nave of Santa Croce with his father and relatives. Grand Duke Ferdinando of Florence directed that he be buried in a tiny room under the bell tower. It wasn't until a hundred years ago that his bones were moved here."

Sunlight flooded the nave. Thomas looked up at the sculpture of

Galileo. The bearded astronomer held a small telescope in his right hand, the other hand rested on a globe.

"She's here, Thomas. Virginia's here, as her father would have wished...very few people know this. Look for yourself, there's no sign on the tomb of her presence. When his body was moved to this tomb her bones were secretly placed next to him, they now rest together."

Jackson started to cry. He couldn't explain it, it was something he'd never done, even when Ellie died. He focused on the globe under Galileo's left hand, moved closer to see if he could find America. Layers of pain seemed to be dropping away. He put his hand on his guide's shoulder. "You're right, Enrico, I need to see with new eyes."

Enrico smiled. "You're well on your way, signore, maybe a total reinvention won't be necessary."

Jackson turned to Enrico. "We can go."

"As you wish, signore." He motioned Thomas back toward the portal.

Enrico would miss his new friend and wondered if he or anyone else would ever hear of the American again. They walked out arm in arm, Italian style. A low mist clung to the hot paving stones in the piazza, cooler now but still warm to the touch. The sky glowed in gradations of azure fading toward a dusty gray. A thin crescent moon floated in the west.

WATERLOO

The house seemed adrift in the hot summer darkness. Candlelight spilled out the windows, catching the lower branches of a lilac, its leaves open to the night sky. Piano notes, barely audible through the thick walls of the brick building, rose and fell as Antonella Cenci worked her way through Chopin's *Nocturne in C-sharp minor, Opus 27.* The melody joined with the night breeze, a passage too beautiful, it seemed, to come from human hands. But it was a distraction at best, a way to get her mind off the day's events. The war had not gone well and in the midst of the country's despair her son had seen fit to enlist. Just then a door slammed on the back porch catching the tail of Antonella's cat.

"Is that you, Fabrizio?"

"Yes, Mama."

"Come here, my son." She turned on the piano bench.

"No, Mama, stay..." He kissed the back of her neck. Fabrizio, an only child, adored his mother but now he could only feel the fear in her body. He sat next to her.

"Tell me...what will happen?" She could hardly form the words. "When do you leave?"

Fabrizio's uncle had told him that in Italy mothers imagine their sons to be the baby Jesus. He could understand; he would always remain the bambino in her eyes. Antonella caressed his cheek with the back of her hand.

"In two weeks...we muster in on August 22." She embraced him, started to cry. It felt like searing hot metal had exploded inside her.

"It's all right, Mama. My friends enlisted with me, we'll take care of each other."

The mother who had been his light now seemed distant, almost a stranger. Fabrizio searched her face; he wanted to understand. Her brown eyes glazed with tears, her face looked old.

She held him tight to keep him safe, to never let him go. "Mama, please, you must be strong, it's the beginning of a grand adventure."

Antonella had grown up in a small village in Sicily and saw cousins and uncles proudly march off to war only to be maimed and slaughtered. It was exactly why Tomaso, her husband, brought the family to the remote village of Waterloo in upstate New York. He had little money, but his stone carving and masonry expertise served him well in the new world. The stories about his apprenticeship near the Carrara marble quarries and his visits to the tomb of his favorite sculptor, Michelangelo, were family legends.

Antonella loosened her grip, sat back, and held her son at arm's-length. The light of the candle on the piano lit the tears on her cheeks. She looked past him, through the window, down Virginia Street where gas lamps illuminated two wagons resting by the curb. The quiet scene reminded her of how peaceful their life had become in the Finger Lakes, how lucky they were to be safe from the violent events unfolding three hundred miles to the south. The thought of her son in battle made her hands tingle.

"Mama, I need you to understand." Her silence unnerved him. Antonella's deep motherly affection had created a son with a warm personality, always sensitive to helping others. It was in his nature to look for a way to ease his mother's discomfort and music called out to him. He shuffled through the piano sheets and found their favorite piece, then smoothed the pages flat, pressing down on the center crease until the folio stayed in place.

"You must relax. Please, let's play." Antonella was Waterloo's only piano teacher and Fabrizio her star pupil. On special occasions they performed together in the front parlor of the Gridley home on Main Street. To hear piano compositions for four hands was a rare treat, so as many as thirty people would crowd into Charles and Eleanora Gridley's brick home to watch mother and son play.

Fabrizio reached over and took his mother's hand. "I'll be safe, please don't worry." The black sweater he wore was knitted by Antonella's mother. It took months for it to arrive by ship but it came loaded with memories. Antonella's father had worn a similar sweater years ago. He was the fabro, the goldsmith of the village. She loved watching him work in his studio, pouring molten metal, extruding and annealing gold sheets, testing old jewelry with nitric acid. He was proudest of his aqua regia, a corrosive mix of hydrochloric and nitric acid with which he could precisely measure the purity of gold. It had been a magical place for a little girl and she wished Fabrizio could have known it. She rubbed his arm, stroked the soft black wool, and then turned to the piano.

For a full minute she kept her eyes closed, imaging the hand positions, the tempo. This was the way she always began Mozart's *Sonata for Piano Duet in C Major, K. 521*, envisioning the entire piece in her mind. When she was ready, she moved her hands above the keys and nodded to Fabrizio. Antonella, seated on the right, began the first bar, picking up the melody, playing the treble, while Fabrizio set the tempo and controlled the pedaling. His hands moved over the keyboard. She never tired of looking at them, hands so large they could easily cover a third of the keys.

Mother and son immersed themselves; they became the music. For the moment there was nothing else, no worries, no war, just the pure art of the sonata. They moved with precision, sliding into the notes, the quarters, the eighths, the sixteenths. Sometimes their hands crossed over each other to their mutual delight. The first semblance of a smile started to cross Antonella's face. They were a perfect match, producing a sublimely harmonious sound.

In the last movement of the piece, Mozart noted a cadenza, a place for performers to improvise. This was Antonella's speciality, a rare skill she always performed to perfection with Fabrizio at her side. He kept the tempo while her original melody danced across the keys. He winked his approval as they returned to the final bars of the composition. When it was finished she turned to him, her eyes fixed on his lips, almost marble-like in their smoothness. A mother could do that, she thought, admire the physical beauty of the being she had produced. For a moment longer she held the joy before the reality of the day washed back over her.

"Here..." Fabrizio hesitated. "Here are my papers." He was as excited and proud about his coming adventure as his mother was terrified. Antonella took the government documents and placed them in the drawer of the side table, as if that would save him. Fabrizio brought over two candles, placed them on the mantelpiece, and sat next to her on the settee.

"I've made your favorite recipe, linguini with pesto and tomato." She only made pesto on the most important occasions. For her, food was love.

"But, Mama, you're too upset, I should be cooking for you!"

"It's no trouble, my son, look." She pointed to the kitchen table. "George brought over all his basil."

"This is too much. You know how long it takes to grind the walnuts and basil." He'd seen her only a few weeks ago working the granite mortar and pestle. "It's not good for your delicate hands; please Mama, save them for the piano."

She reached out to stroke his hair. "It's done, and look, I only have one blister."

"You treat me too good."

"I never ask you anything, Fabrizio." She hesitated, rubbed her sore thumb. "But this, do this for me...for yourself...stay."

"It's what I need to do." He looked away, tried to remain cheerful, hoped it might change her mind. "I've joined the 33rd Regiment, we've been put in Company C...Ken and John and everyone else from Waterloo will be with me."

"My God, Fabrizio, they took Ken, he's only sixteen!"

"Yes, Mama, he told them he was seventeen, like me."

She ran her hands up and down her thighs. "Promise me you will be careful, you must stay with your friends, those you can trust to..." But she could not finish, her body trembled and her hands began to shake.

"Listen, Mama, the recruiter told us we'd be in no danger since we outnumber the Rebs two to one. Look at me. I'm strong, healthy, and almost six feet tall, who's gonna hurt me!"

Antonella reached for the drawer, took the papers, and started to read. Her eyes stuck on the words *two year enlistment*. "Oh no, Fabrizio, what have you done?"

"What now?"

"Two years!" She held up the papers and pointed. "I'll never see you again!"

"Please, Mama, it won't be two years. Everyone says the war will be over this year..." He moved to embrace her.

"Mary's son signed up for one year."

"The captain encouraged us to enlist for two years, but he said the Rebs would be whipped in no time."

Antonella ached to tell him more, but it was too late, it would do no good to frighten Fabrizio. She hugged him and cried.

"He's an officer, he knows how superior we are..." Fabrizio released his embrace. "Please, listen to me, the Confederates don't even have proper uniforms, many are barefoot...it can't last long."

She sat back. A moonbeam slanted down through the open parlor window and illuminated his forehead and eyes. The sound of the evening breeze passing through the pine branches high above distracted her for a moment. She remembered Fabrizio in her arms, wrapped in a woolen blanket, suckling her nipple. He had been a happy baby, easy to raise, full of love...and now, the war. She wasn't sure if she could keep breathing.

"Mama, please, I'll be home by Christmas..."

SAVAGES STATION

The sorrel gelding stood in the middle of the clearing, content to be on dry ground. The rider, Major General Thomas J. "Stonewall" Jackson, was even more content. He had spent three miserable days struggling to respond to General Robert E. Lee's directives and the results, by his own estimation, had been pitifully sluggish and uncoordinated. Jackson had been brought in from the west to assist in Lee's effort to turn back the Union Army moving up the Virginia Peninsula toward Richmond. After his great victories in the Shenandoah Valley, Jackson had earned the respect of the entire Confederacy, but in late June of 1862 the swamps and rivers just to the east of Richmond had reduced his command to frustration and misery. Everywhere he turned there was more water than enemy. Totopotomoy, Chickahominy, Mattaponi, Pamunkey, and so on...he'd never seen such names for rivers and couldn't imagine how a person would pronounce them.

"Sergeant, we'll hold here till the scouts tell us what's to the south, there's a mighty lot of commotion coming from that direction."

"Two batteries stuck bad in the river bottom, good thing we're stopping, General."

"How's that bridge coming, Sergeant?" The general moved to slap a cluster of chiggers on his wrist. "Can't understand what Lee's thinking, asking us to build bridges instead of chasing Yanks!"

"Another few hours, sir..."

"Another what?" Jackson was tired, bone tired, and wasn't thinking straight. His hair needed a good brushing and his boots were way past repair.

"Hours, sir...You asked about the bridge...it'll be another few hours, the Chickahominy waters are swollen, currents moving like a pack of wild cats."

"Send for Lieutenant Baker. I need to know what's in front of us."

"Sir, our lead scouts just reported they sighted Savages Station in the distance. General Magruder's engaged there against several Yankee divisions."

"A fine name that is...What am I to make of this country? Boatswain's Swamp, Turkey Bridge, Fort Darling, and now Savages Station. I 'spect we'll find some extra-fierce Yankees there!" Jackson was too tired to laugh at his own joke; he'd gone four days without sleep and wanted nothing more than a dry bed.

"Here's Lieutenant Baker!" called out the sergeant. The young officer saluted, then brushed off his uniform with a dirty glove. He had a baby face, and could have been mistaken for a choir boy except for his crude mouth.

"Damn, what a fine muddy mess you are, Lieutenant, looks like those Union savages whooped ya ass." The sergeant started to laugh, then thought better of it. The lieutenant, a favorite of Jackson's, wasn't used to the jesting that came with the general's affection.

"Well, sir," began the lieutenant, "I wish I could've presented a better appearance, but them son a bitch swamps we be racin' through need some serious fixing!"

Jackson grunted, too tired to smile. "Ya got any good news?" He turned his head and spat on the ground, then wiped a worn sleeve across his greasy forehead. "Tell us you found me some enemy...been slogging through swamp and bog for near four days and still haven't cut off the Yanks."

"Sir, if we stop building bridges and move along I think we gonna catch us a pile of Yanks, they be lying everywhere up ahead."

"How you mean that, son?"

"I mean, they be sick, wounded, thousands of them...smells like stinkin' hell in Savages Station, turns your nose from near a mile away."

The general just stared at him, figured the lieutenant was more tired then he was. "Ya mean they're marching the wounded away?"

"No, sir, they're just lying in shit and bandages...I think the Yanks deserted them, just up and left...There's abandoned weapons thrown everywhere." The lieutenant punched at his neck but it was too late, a bright red mosquito bite dripped blood onto his collar.

"We'll see soon enough." Jackson squinted into the bright haze to the west. "Sun's too low to move the division now...send word to Whiting and Hill to find high ground and set up for the night." With that the general swung his right leg over the saddle and jumped to the ground. He handed off his horse to the sergeant, then loosened his belt and scratched a sore on his hip. Off to his left he heard the wings of an owl cutting through the air. "I'm staying here, it's the driest patch I've seen since we left the Shenandoah Valley." He threw his hat down for a pillow and curled into a ball on the piney forest floor.

* * *

Smoke hung like a soiled blanket, just high enough off the ground to increase the misery of the gathered sick, but Fabrizio had other problems. He could no longer control his temperature. It had spiked up and down for two days. At the moment he was shivering uncontrollably in ninety-eight degree heat even though he had pulled a damp coat over his head.

Nearly three thousand patients lay scattered along the Richmond and York River Railroad at Savages Station. A lucky few lay in tents and sheds, but most, like Fabrizio, suffered on the sun-baked ground. The Henrico County summer had been much too hot and as July approached, the humidity and biting insect levels had exploded to the upside.

"I'm looking for Corporal Fabrizio Cenci."

"Can't help ya, Sergeant," snapped the orderly. "We've been ordered to evacuate."

"Just point me to the New York Infantry." The sergeant tried to hold his temper; he'd never met an orderly he liked. As far as he was concerned they were all failed soldiers forced into medical duty to keep them out of the way.

The orderly half smiled at the sergeant. "I guess the quickest way to get ya outta my face is to point over there." He raised his arm slowly, as if it were the hardest thing he'd ever done. "By the cedar trees, there's a group from New York."

Fabrizio heard him coming and tried to wave, but he couldn't move his arm. He'd been on his back all day, exhausted, dehydrated, covered with bites. The diarrhea had started in May after his squad drank from a pond contaminated with runoff from the regimental latrines. All the men had come down with loose bowels but most recovered in a few days. Not Fabrizio, it had become chronic, it was killing him.

"So here you are, Fabrizio." The sergeant tried to sound cheerful but was shaken by the sight of the sick soldier. Fabrizio, a robust, healthy young man in Waterloo, now looked like living death. "I'm sorry it's been difficult for you, my friend."

"I had such high hopes, Eric..." he whispered. "When we left Waterloo we were full of ourselves... *Bring on the Rebs* you screamed. Remember the first weeks, we bonded like brothers..."

"Closer than brothers...remember in Arlington when we lined up behind the headquarters tent and bet dimes who could piss the farthest?" The sergeant smiled, then held his hands as far apart as possible to indicate the distance. "This is how much most of us could reach but you... you were double that distance!"

Fabrizio tried to laugh but it hurt too much. "Now look at us, Sergeant. I'm half dead and the rest of the company's beat to hell." He started to cough, then reached out to the sergeant with a wet hand. "Help me up, I'm too weak to..."

"No, no, it's best you stay here." He was unrecognizable as the man Sergeant Brown had hunted with on weekends in Waterloo. Fabrizio's blue eyes had turned gray, his skin was pasty and hung loose.

"I'm so thirsty..." Fabrizio tried to move again but collapsed in a spasm of coughing. "Some water...please..."

The smell of the field hospital turned the sergeant's stomach. Old sweat, feces, clotted blood, and severed limbs had baked in the sun for days. The foul air was way past description; perhaps it was what desperation and numb resignation were supposed to smell like. Even worse was the retching and vomiting of men trying to clear the acrid smoke from their lungs. The sergeant wanted no more of it. Desperate for a cloth to block the smell he held his kepi tight against his face.

"Let me see if I can find you something to drink." The sergeant knew there would be water a mile up the tracks and it was a good excuse to get away.

"Please, don't leave..."

"You need water, I'll be right back." The sergeant shook with fear.

69

He wanted to move away, well aware that disease was a greater danger than the enemy. There had been rumors that smallpox was making its way among the sick and wounded. Everywhere he looked men were suffering, some wet with fever, others gasping for breath. He was surrounded by malaria, typhoid fever, pneumonia, mumps, measles, and the dreaded pox. Best to get away.

"Take me with you."

"I'm sorry..."

"Why have you come?" Fabrizio tried to prop himself up on his elbow but it brought on another coughing spasm. Sergeant Brown stepped back, pushing his hat closer to his mouth.

"I came to bring you this." He reached into his pocket and pulled out a soiled envelope. "It's from Antonella."

Fabrizio turned it slowly in his hand. "Please...please read it to me." He touched the paper to his nose then dropped it on his chest.

The sergeant hesitated to take the envelope back, he knew Antonella well, knew how close Fabrizio was to his mother. "Maybe you should hold it a bit, read it yourself...later." The sergeant imagined Antonella in her kitchen cooking rosemary chicken for Fabrizio and his friends. "I'm sorry, Fabrizio, I wish we all could be back home." His own mother's Irish cooking was adequate but nothing to brag about. He preferred Antonella's table.

"When are we moving, Sergeant?"

"Not now, you're staying here."

"Here...the Rebs are coming!"

"Some are staying...the sick...the wounded." The sergeant looked away. "Our orders are to move before Stonewall gets here."

"But you came for me..."

"I came to say goodbye."

"Eric...please..." Fabrizio fell back exhausted, "I can't see you.... hold my hand, tell me what's happening?"

The sergeant kneeled, took Fabrizio's right hand. "General McClellan has fled...left no one in charge. Our orders are to burn everything, then move toward the James River. Jackson's division is just down the road, there's no time left..." As he spoke Fabrizio's hand went cold and damp.

"You're leaving me to the Rebs?"

"The rear guard is here..." The sergeant could hardly speak, his words tumbled out in a low tone. "...We've been holding up the Confederates while the main army escapes through the swamps...the captain just ordered the rest of us out."

"Who'll protect us?"

The sergeant had no answer. "I have to go, Fabrizio." He squeezed the cold hand then placed it gently on the grass.

"Some water...please help me."

The sergeant remembered he had a half-empty canteen on his belt. He unscrewed the cap and poured a small amount of musty water into Fabrizio's mouth but it only caused him to cough. "Here, keep it until someone comes." He placed the canteen between Fabrizio's legs, then wiped some flies off his forehead. "You'll be all right..." Across the tracks he saw crows pulling flesh off a corpse.

"Don't leave me...Eric...please." He turned his head to see the sergeant but there was no one there.

*　*　*

"Through here, watch your step." The guide held the torch high against the bricks of the arch so Jackson wouldn't hit his head. The Colosseum seemed much higher than he had expected. In the moonlight, rows of seats climbed halfway to the heavens. The Roman night was soft, a breeze flowed through chinks in the bricks and dropped dust into the guide's flame. Venus floated low in the inky sky, just above a broken column.

"Where are all the people, there's no one here?"

"They're dead, you know that, signore, lions ate them, every last one!"

"I don't understand..." Lightning flashed and it started to rain. Strange, thought Jackson, not a cloud in the sky and my clothes are drenched. Someone shook his shoulder.

"Sir, it's almost midnight," whispered Lieutenant Baker, "wind's picking up."

"What…what are you doing here?"

"You asked me to wake you…remember…when the scouts returned."

"Oh my…been dreaming I was back in Rome."

"Sounds good, hope the weather's better there."

"Hell of a lot better than this." Jackson found himself in a muddy pool of water with slashing rain blowing in from the west. He jumped up and tried to slap the water off his pants but it was no use, he was soaked through. The Virginia Peninsula was as close to hell as he would ever get. The roads were rutted and slippery, the swamps exuded foul airs, and the noisome insects and searing temperatures seemed to increase by the minute. By day the broiling air left a man ready to scream, at night the humid miasma turned the soldiers into wilted and irritable victims of the river bottoms.

"What day is it?" Jackson mumbled, his mind still half in Rome.

"June 29, sir. In a few minutes it'll be the 30th."

"Oh my…"

"What, sir?"

"June 29, it's a big holiday in Italy, feast of Saints Peter and Paul." He looked up at the sky, then continued. "Had my best meal in Europe on June 29 at an inn near the Tiber."

"Could of used a meal like that last night, sir…"

"If I remember right the wine was white…" Jackson stared into the lieutenant's eyes. "But enough of that, tell me what's happening."

"Scouts say the Federals have abandoned Savages Station. All that's left is the field hospital, weapons scattered everywhere."

"Must of been in a big hurry to get somewhere."

"If ya don't mind me saying I 'spect they be worried General Jackson's gonna catch em!"

"Put out the word to move, no sense trying to sleep in this." A gust of warm air blew out of the stand of pines to his left and turned his mind back to Rome. Since he left Lexington in March, he had totally forgotten about his time in the Mediterranean. His new wife, Anna, had asked him about his European trip. He'd promised her they would go to Italy when the fighting was over. It had been his favorite place.

"Sir, it'll take about an hour to form the units, the dark and the storms be slowing things down."

"That's fine, son, so long as we're in Savages Station by first light..." Jackson paused, still too tired to think straight. The rain let up for a moment and through a patch in the clouds the moon tried to break free. "When the picket lines are ready to move let me know...I'll wait here." He knelt down to pray but he couldn't stop thinking of his wife's smile, her embrace when he said they'd be going to Italy. The sweet memory only served to remind him how homesick he was. He didn't pray for victory, he just wanted the killing to end. In the distance the familiar rattle of mess gear, confused cussing and the hitching of horses invaded his prayers. He squeezed his eyes tighter and prayed to be home...soon.

* * *

Fabrizio focused on the sky. The desperate sound of the hundreds that lay helpless in the dark washed over him, kept him awake. A steady rain began after midnight, but now and then he caught a glimpse of the stars. He lay on his back soaking up the muddy earth, his mouth opened wide to drink in as much of the heavenly gift as the storms would provide. The milk-warm rain slackened his thirst and calmed his fevered mind. He concentrated on one thing: how to drag himself away from the enemy.

He flopped an arm onto the leg of the man to his left. "Who's this?" he whispered. There was no answer so he squeezed the thigh muscle to wake him. The flesh, rigid under the wool trousers, felt like cool steel. Clasped in one hand of the corpse was a faded photo of a young woman with an infant. Fabrizio tried to move to see it better but only managed to knock his canteen onto the stomach of the man on his right.

"Thank ya, friend."

"I'm sorry...didn't mean to..."

"Don't be sorry, I needed a drink...whiskey would have been better..."

"Can you help me up?" Fabrizio rolled his body toward the man.

"Wish I could but..."

"Oh no..." gasped Fabrizio. The man was a double amputee with a head wound wrapped in blood-encrusted bandages. A trail of ants worked its way up his neck. Fabrizio moved to wipe off the insects but his hand wouldn't reach that far.

"I took shrapnel at Boatswain's Creek. We got stuck in the swamp and the Reb artillery knocked the crap out of us...been bleeding here ever since... the son a bitch surgeons cut my legs off!"

Fabrizio rolled onto his back. "Been rotting here for three days, got the dysentery a month ago."

"Ya planning to run...don't look like you'll get far, friend."

"We've been left to die, haven't we?"

"And here you'll stay, I wish you luck." The soldier took another drink from the canteen, then tossed it back. "Tell ya what, Corporal, maybe ya best crawl away fast, otherwise the Rebs gonna throw ya in a trench an kick in some dirt."

"I'm not dead yet!" Fabrizio snapped back. He looked at the the amputee's uniform and saw he was a busted sergeant. Newly sewn corporal stripes barely covered where the sergeant patches had been ripped off.

Fabrizio propped himself up on his elbows, then with great effort sat up. The sky was beginning to show the first blush of dawn. Warm, smoky air drifted here and there in a listless breeze that couldn't clear the noxious clouds.

"What's on the grass?" asked the soldier.

"Hand it to me, it's a letter my sergeant brought."

The soldier nodded. "There's something in it, you're a lucky man."

Fabrizio felt the envelope. "Look," he said, then tore the end of the envelope, "there's two biscotti wrapped in parchment, one for each of us. My mother makes them with honey, cinnamon, and almonds."

"No, thanks." He pointed to his mouth. "Lookie, not a tooth left."

Fabrizio put one of the biscotti in his pocket and started to chew on the smaller one. The envelope was blue parchment with a Geneva, NY, postmark. He rubbed his thumb across the address written in brown ink.

"I think they're coming," whispered the soldier with a hand to his ear, "there'll be hell to pay now!"

Fabrizio felt faint.

"Breathe, Corporal, you're holding your breath."

It had been deadly still, now there was a stir in the distance, crows squawking, hawks circling over the western woods where the Rebel pickets were sure to appear. Behind the birds a waning gibbous moon shone just over the tree tops, its color pale vermillion. Chills worked their way up Fabrizio's spine. He struggled to gulp in the smoky air, then unfolded the letter.

> *My Dearest Fabrizio,*
>
> *I was so happy to receive your last letter of May 31. You know well how disappointed I was that you did not return for Christmas as you had promised. But now I take great comfort in your prediction that the summer campaign in Virginia will result in the taking of Richmond and the end of the fighting. It is all that I pray for. I am glad to hear that the troops admire General McClellan and trust that he will lead you to an early victory.*
>
> *But the greatest relief is to hear you are well. We read in the papers the most frightening stories of injury and disease afflicting so many of the men. It gives us great comfort to know that your fellow townsmen are there to watch over you.*
>
> *I send along these biscotti as a reminder of what awaits your early return. The army food must be terribly difficult for you. I can't wait to see your face when you taste my lasagna again!*
>
> *You know how deeply your father and I love you. We could not bear to hear that even the smallest thing has harmed you. We have kept a candle burning on the piano since the afternoon you left and Father Kelly says a prayer for you and all the men during mass.*
>
> *My sweet son, may our ever loving God protect you and deliver you safely to us.*
>
> *Mille Baci,*
>
> *Mama*
>
> *15 June 1862*

* * *

"Never seen anything like it, Sergeant." General Jackson had proven his ability to kill Yankees, but the mass of helpless Union soldiers that lay before his eyes threw him off his game. He shook his head and pointed toward a group of amputees propped against a wall near the tracks. "Don't imagine those poor souls have much good to say about their General McClellan."

"Sir, our scouts have found a Union supply depot but there's nothing left, they burned it all... powder, guns, provisions, even the bandages and medicine for these men."

"Been trying to catch McClellan for near a week, Sergeant, and look what he leaves us, smoke and disease!" Jackson dismounted and walked among the sick. He tried not to look at the faces, there was too much pain in their stares and he couldn't afford the distraction. The rain had stopped, but water still dripped off the cedar trees onto the wounded. "Lieutenant, bring up the chaplain, I reckon he's got some work here."

Fabrizio saw the Rebel group walking toward him but had no idea who they were. Surrounded by the enemy, he expected things to go bad fast. His hunting friends had warned him to never stare a dangerous animal in the eye, so he looked away. His legs started to tremble even though the early morning temperature was pushing ninety. He struggled to breathe.

General Jackson, at nearly six feet and 175 pounds, was larger than the average soldier but that was hardly enough to account for the impression he made when he stepped into Fabrizio's averted field of vision. Jackson looked nothing like a Union commander. He was roughly dressed with musty, wet pants, a private's hat, and eyes that burned with the fervor Fabrizio had come to fear when he heard stories of the Rebels. If he had known he was in the presence of the great Confederate commander he probably would have come unhinged. Or if he had known that both Jackson and his own father had once stood before the tomb of Michelangelo, not at the same time, but with equal reverence, he might have relaxed a bit in wonder that they had shared such a distant experience. Or if he had been whole and not deathly sick, maybe he would have tried to kill the general. But none of that happened. Instead he turned his face up and spoke.

"Good morning, sir..." he began, fearful he would be struck. "I have little to offer, but the soldier here has no teeth and could not eat this biscotti my mother sent me." With the little strength remaining in his body he held the cookie out. "Perhaps, if you like it, you will spare our lives." Fabrizio's hand shook but he forced it toward Jackson, then dared to look straight into the Rebel's blue eyes for a response.

Jackson showed nothing, but in his war-ravaged mind, deep emotions were struggling to the surface. He stared at the pathetic figure on the ground, uniform soiled, dirt and leaves in his hair, a face so ashen it seemed death had already wrapped its arms around him.

"Where's your mama from, Corporal?"

"Sicily, near Cefalu, sir, a bit east of Palermo, she's the best cook… always serves Vin Santo with her biscotti."

The general took the biscotti, held it up to the sun for a moment, then took a bite. The rough texture of the almonds, mingled with the bright flavor of Italian cinnamon and honey, took him straight back to his days in Florence. He could hear Enrico pouring the Vin Santo, saw the candles he lit for Ellie, smelled the lilies in the Boboli Gardens.

"It's good, son, mighty obliged." Jackson wanted to say more but he was fighting to control himself. The strain of a week of sleepless nights, the frustration of losing the enemy in the rain-swollen swamps, the absurdity of the helpless group of Yankees laid out before him, brought his emotions to a place he'd never been.

"A drink of water, sir, just a drink…" Fabrizio asked, then fell back, exhausted.

The general knelt down and reached back. "Sergeant, hand me a canteen." He'd never touched a Yankee before and hesitated for a moment before cradling Fabrizio's head. He felt the corporal's emaciated torso, how easy it was to lift the disease-ravaged body. He moved the canteen to Fabrizio's mouth.

"I think he's gone, sir." Jackson turned toward the lieutenant. "Here, let me help you." They lowered Fabrizio's head down onto the grass. Stonewall removed the letter grasped in Fabrizio's left hand, then arranged the corporal's arms together on his stomach. The lieutenant reached down and passed his hand over Fabrizio's face to close the eyelids. It was strange, Jackson thought, he wanted to pray for the corporal but it would have to wait.

"See that this man gets a proper burial," he whispered. The words came out automatically but Jackson knew the lieutenant wouldn't understand. Fabrizio had won the general's heart, had touched his deepest memories. He looked down at Fabrizio and saw the lost son of an Italian mother. His mind filled with images of his sister Elizabeth and his own son. It struck him how much sadder was Fabrizio's fate, lost forever in the midst of his enemies. For a moment he imagined Fabrizio interred in a grand Renaissance tomb in memory of the men from North and South who had died alone, unknown. He could see the marbles, the sculptures, the incense, the gathered priests. It would be grand and fitting, he would see to that. He even knew the words he would say from the altar in the moments before Fabrizio's mother would lay a single white lily on the stone sarcophagus and kiss the cool stone. Yes, it should be that way, he thought.

"Sir, we need to move, there's firing off to our left." As usual, Jackson needed to be reminded that danger was near. The staccato sound of rifle fire hadn't registered in his mind but an artillery round passing overhead caught his attention. Jackson moved toward his horse, then turned back for a moment.

"Lieutenant, the corporal deserves a proper grave, do what you can."

CODA

General Jackson caught up with the rear elements of the Union Army later that day in the quagmire of White Oak Swamp, but he was able to get only one division into action before the Yankees slipped away again. The following afternoon, in a final attempt to catch the Union Army, Lee and the rest of the Confederate commanders were drawn into a disastrous encounter at Malvern Hill. The Rebels lost over 6,000 men in a few hours and never regained momentum. This ended General Lee's offensive effort to cut off and destroy the Northern army before they reached the James River. McClellan's Peninsula Campaign had cost both sides dearly (16,000 Union and 20,000 Confederate casualties). The Yankees, driven away from their attempt to take Richmond, had nothing to show for their effort. The Confederates at least had saved their capital and found a new commander in General Lee.

Back in Savages Station, the Confederates did their best to bury the Union dead at the field hospital abandoned by McClellan. The bodies were collected in shallow trench graves around the site. In a search a few years after the war's end only 269 Union soldiers were found and exhumed for reburial at Seven Pines National Cemetery near Richmond. None of the relatives of those lost at Savages Station were ever notified of the location of their dead. Most were never found. The few bodies located remain unidentified and their graves are all marked unknown.

With the threat to Richmond neutralized, Lee sent Jackson north. His reputation continued to grow as he regained his winning ways at the Second Battle of Bull Run, Harper's Ferry, and Antietam. In May of 1863 he was back in Virginia at the Battle of Chancellorsville. Only sixty-odd miles and eleven months separated him from the difficult days of Savages Station. In the most brilliant moment of his military service, Jackson's corps executed a near impossible flanking maneuver at Chancellorsville and routed the Union Army on May 2. It should have been the greatest day of his career, but fate intervened. While returning to his headquarters he was mistaken in the dark for Union cavalry and shot three times by sentries of the 18th North Carolina Infantry. During his evacuation he was accidentally dropped off a stretcher, then endured amputation of his left arm. He lingered with pneumonia for several more difficult days before dying on May 10. His body was moved to the Governor's Mansion in Richmond for a short period of public viewing, then buried near his wife's home in Lexington, deep in the Shenandoah Valley.

What came next has confounded and confused most right-thinking Americans ever since, but it probably would have been understandable to Jackson and certainly to Fabrizio's mother. After all, Jackson had spent time in Italy and had come to appreciate the love the Italians had for the remains of their saints and artists. How could he forget Florence's successful effort to steal the body of Michelangelo from Rome or the clandestine attempt to remove Dante's body from Ravenna? The love for Jackson throughout the Confederacy was great, but it was especially intense among those who soldiered with him. Jackson's chaplain, the Reverend Lacy, was in a unique position to act on this devotion. He took Jackson's arm, wrapped it in a blanket, and buried it in the family cemetery on the Ellwood plantation, less than a mile from the Chancellorsville field hospital where the arm had been amputated. A small granite monument was placed over the burial spot inscribed with the words *Arm of Stonewall Jackson May 3, 1863*.

A year later, during the Battle of the Wilderness, the soldiers of the North and South found themselves fighting once again near Lacy Cemetery. The Ellwood plantation served as a Union headquarters and during their stay Jackson's arm was exhumed out of curiosity by the Northern troops, then reburied. There it rested until 1921 when Marine General Smedley Butler came upon the marker. Doubting the veracity of the words on the granite he ordered his men to dig up the ground to prove there was no arm there. The general was so embarrassed when the arm appeared that he ordered it reburied. There it remains, the object of veneration by thousands of annual visitors who seek out the cemetery to pay homage to the general who once stood before the tomb of Michelangelo.

Part Three

CENOTAPH

You shall find out how salt is the taste of another man's bread, and how hard is the way up and down another man's stairs.

DANTE

Prelude

The river shows the way. It seems to widen with each bend, first past Philadelphia, then Chester and Raccoon Island, as if it knows it will become a sea. High above, a great blue heron moves her wings in graceful thrusts against the summer wind. Her legs float straight back in perfect alignment with the river. Below Wilmington, two massive steel structures slow the journey for both the heron and the rush of human traffic flowing up and down the East coast. The soaring towers of the Delaware Memorial Bridges force the heron up, high enough to see what the human travelers cannot, a tear-shaped island in the middle of the Delaware, just downriver. From the bridge deck, 174 feet above the Delaware, the island is blocked from human view, hidden by the Jersey banks where the river turns and heads east toward the open waters of Delaware Bay and the Atlantic.

Gliding down from high above the traffic, the heron trims her wings, slows the descent, points toward the island where she hopes to find a lost mate. She settles in a few feet above the river and flies toward the pointed northern end of the island. Her wings push air against the water, giving extra lift, lightening the effort. The smell of the sea calms her.

She alights in the shallows just off the neck of the island and spears a young blueback herring. The long slender fish, with sparkling silver scales and frightened eyes, struggles for a moment then disappears into the bird. Like a mother who feels something wrong when a son dies in a distant war, the heron senses trouble. Perhaps it's the bleached scapula half imbedded in a nearby dune, or maybe it's the massive stone building looming through the trees to the south...or maybe it's just a certain tang in the air. The bird knows the ancient scent of death.

PRINCETON - SPRING 1835

May 15, 1835

Perry Town, Maryland

My Dear Son James,

I wish your mother and I could have joined you at graduation. How disappointed you must be. As you know, the planting season has been delayed for weeks with all the rain we received in April. Finally, the ground has dried enough for the slaves to work the fields and, God willing, the tobacco seedlings will be in soon. Unfortunately, that's the least of it for we've had great trouble with the slaves. Two males escaped a week ago and the slave catchers tracked them as far as Philadelphia only to lose them when they waded across the Schuylkill in a storm. We whipped their women but none would talk. Perhaps they had nothing to hide, who knows. As if that were not enough, your mother has been overwhelmed with birthing babies in the slave quarters. Her midwifery skills have saved more than one baby this month, but five were lost. It is as if all the negroes arranged to deliver during the planting season. I regret now having given the help so much time off after the summer harvest. One baby was a breech birth and would surely have died if Mother hadn't been able to reach in, untangle the cord and turn the body around. He came out fine but not before the woman exhausted herself with screaming. We named him Jeremiah and I must say he is a happy little darkie. It seemed like the perfect name for a baby who prevailed over certain death in the womb. The house slaves told us that Jeremiah means "Yahweh exalts" so we all took pleasure in that.

We look forward to your safe return and are so proud of your accomplishments.

Your loving Father

James Bacon folded the letter four times and slipped the rough edged vellum inside his black robe. It had been a long ceremony and none of the speeches held his attention. *Funny,* he thought, *bright students and even more brilliant professors everywhere, but it's the insects I'll remember.* Laid out on the great lawn before Nassau Hall were neat rows of chairs for students, faculty and guests. Everyone had assembled at noon to honor the new graduates, but the natural world intervened.

It was the thirteenth year in the cicada life cycle. High above, forty feet up in the white oaks, thousands of newly emerged cicadas clicked and clacked, their drone rising and falling in a cacophonous roar. The volume rose with the temperature, now near one hundred. James brushed back his hair. He knew that he would be one of the first to receive a diploma.

"James Bacon, Bachelor of Arts," called out the Provost, looking up into the trees as if it might calm the insects, "please step forward."

James rose, noticed the moon still visible in the sky. It reminded him of his favorite class, Renaissance Studies. He had learned much over the past four years, most of it lost or hidden away in notebooks, but he would never forget October, 1582. He could still hear the professor explaining that popes could do mostly what they wanted back then. Pope Gregory XIII outdid them all when he announced that the ten days following October 4, 1582 would be eliminated in order to adjust for the Julian calendar's inaccuracies. He declared that the day after October 4 was October 15 and that was that. Too bad if you had a birthday or anniversary on October 10, you would just have to wait until 1583.

James walked past the faculty section, then climbed the stone steps to the dais. The slate tread at the top was a little off and he scraped one toe of his perfectly polished shoes. He bent down to smooth the smudge and felt something hit his head. The molting had begun. Pieces of the insects' shedding skin poured down upon the gathering.

He moved ahead and reached out to accept his diploma just as a large cicada dropped inside the open end of the rolled parchment. The Provost knocked the diploma against the lectern but the insect would not budge. The audience started to laugh and so did James, but not for the same reason. He was thinking of his parents and how displeased his mother would have been. She had a deadly fear of bugs and the vibrating cicada inside his diploma, with two huge green eyes protruding from the side of the head, and three smaller eyes in between, would have put the fear into her. James tried to look serious but the harder he tried the more he smiled. He imagined that his mother surely would have been running across the campus, looking for the quickest way out of Princeton.

Why did I come out of the womb to see toil and sorrow,
and spend my days in shame?

JEREMIAH 20:18

Delaware Bay - Fall 1863

The bay spread before Jeremiah like a great sea. In the far distance, off to the right, he could just make out the lavender shadow of Cape May. To the south, on the horizon, the Delaware shore loomed, a neutral grey like the rebel uniforms he expected to find in abundance ahead. He stood on the forecastle of the square-rigged frigate USS Washington, his hand on the gunwale to steady himself as the ship cut through the sloppy Atlantic chop. It was autumn of 1863, two years into the Rebellion. The sergeant shaded his eyes with his free hand and peered into the distance. There was only water ahead, no sign of where the bay ended and the river began.

It was all new to Jeremiah. He had never been on a ship before, never seen the world from the water, never felt so alive. He sensed that there just might be another world, a place where he could look forward to better times and so he relaxed, for the first time in his short life. The grand vista calmed him to such a degree that for the next few minutes he allowed himself to replay in his mind the hellish existence he had endured over the past twenty years.

Born into slavery in Maryland, he knew by the age of ten that lost love was life's expected condition, that violence was the frequent reward for endless days of toil, and early death the only reprieve from constant suffering. When Jeremiah was five his father had been caught taking damaged apples from the ground and whipped until his back and arms were a pulpy mess. He died of tetanus two weeks later. Jeremiah tried to block the horror of it, but the pain endured. His mother, sold to a Virginia planter, disappeared from his life when he was nine.

KNOW ALL MEN BY THESE PRESENTS, That I John Ba-
con, of the Village of Perry Town and State of Maryland, for and
in consideration of the sum of four hundred dollars, have granted,
bargained and sold a Negro Woman by name Hany supposed to be
between twenty five and thirty years of age, about five feet tall and
very dark complexion, a slave for life TO HAVE AND TO HOLD
the said described Negro Woman unto Deke Mugby of Virginia his
Executors, Administrators and Assigns forever...

The next seven years offered little better. Jeremiah was a child living as an adult. The loss of his parents crushed what little spirit he had
left, leaving him empty, barren of the spark that keeps most of us going
when all seems lost. If there had been a cliff he would have walked off
it, but the flat Maryland landscape offered no easy way out. The other
slaves avoided him and it was then that James Bacon, home ten years
from Princeton, noticed he had a problem.

James attended law school after graduation but lawyering never
appealed to him. Running the plantation was what he did best and so,
after he passed the bar, he returned home. His parents, too old to operate
a large slave operation, welcomed him with great relief. Before long he
had taken over the entire enterprise and tobacco production increased.
He was a less harsh taskmaster than his father but it could not be said
it was pleasant to be a slave on the plantation or that severe punishment
ended.

When James saw Jeremiah and the rest of the servants avoiding
each other he moved quickly to solve the problem in his carefully cal-
ibrated operation. The standard solution would have been to sell the
troubled slave but James hesitated, his best laborer was not so easily dis-
posed. A strong young worker like Jeremiah would bring a good price,
but James had favored him after the cruel death of his father and hoped
to protect him. So it was all the more devastating for Jeremiah when
James was offered an inordinately high sum from a Mississippi planter.
Jeremiah always wondered how long his master considered the offer, but
it must not have been long, for within a week Jeremiah was headed to
Vicksburg.

"Press down harder, I wanna see mud squishing ya toes!"

"Yasuh, massa, be doing dat."

"Hey boy, over thar, get back ta work, we be buildin' a courthouse, what ta hell ya upto."

It had been a long time since so many slaves gathered in the center of Vicksburg and it created quite a stir. Some locals likened it to the building of the pyramids but that would be an exaggeration since there were only a hundred or so slaves at the work site. Many of the residents were Baptists and saw most things in Biblical terms which meant they would, on occasion, enhance their stories.

"Tell me when that clay go smooth on ya toes...hear me, boy, what's ya be called?"

"Jeremiah."

"Jeremiah, now that's a big name ain't it now, ya best live up to it, boy."

"Yasuh, boss."

The foreman picked at his teeth to loosen a shred of pork left over from lunch then turned and dribbled it onto the ground. "Ya niggers git movin', nuf talkin'."

The slaves had been preparing the clay since sunup, spreading wet earth on the ground, pouring buckets of water, working it with their feet. It was slippery business. Whenever a slave lost his footing in the sloppy kneading pit the onlookers screamed with laughter and yelled for more. What looked humorous to the local citizens was dangerous for the workers. Sharp stone shards in the clay bloodied their feet as they pressed down. Even worse, it slashed their hands and faces when they fell. The blood in the clay mix added a rusty color to the fired bricks. People assumed that the old trick of withholding oxygen during the firing process accounted for the deep color of the courthouse walls, but the slaves knew better, it was their blood.

"Come here, boy."

"Me?"

"You, that's who I pointing to ain't it?"

"Here I be."

"Y'all know how to work the molds don't ya boy, we needing to get some better speed on the brick pressing."

"Yessuh, I do good."

"I'm trusting ya, boy, git over there an' show me some extra bricks today, ya hear?"

"I be going..."

Jeremiah moved out of the clay slop and headed to the brick pressing machines. He was ecstatic. Brick pressing was a skill that required close contact with the masters. It offered a chance to build trust, to get more freedom at the site and with just a little more leeway he'd be gone, a man on the run, but a free one.

"Here boy, git over here, help me with this mold."

"Move it like dis, it be better dat way."

"Whoa, boy, you good now ain't ya! Hey Johnny, I reckon we got us a smart nigger here." The boss liked Jeremiah because of his appearance and the quiet respect he seemed to show the white masters. He had a classic African face with high cheeks and a strong jaw line. His deep brown skin was flawless, his eyes had the noble gleam of a Nubian king.

"Y'all listen to this here black boy, he some then else!"

Jeremiah demonstrated how to slop the clay into the mold in the way he'd done with his father. The foreman knew right away it would speed up production.

"War ya been learning such thangs boy?"

"Mary's Land boss." His mind went to the shanty he had been raised in. Mary's Land they always called it. His father was the rare Catholic slave in a world steeped in superstition, witch doctors and voodoo. His dad loved Mary and prayed to her every night when they gathered at the broken pine table for the supper scraps the masters sent down. *Jesus is the Lord*, he always began, *but it's Mary who'll save us.* Jeremiah thought that his father must have been talking about some other world because Mary had been no help to them on Earth.

"Johnny, git your ass over here, I told ya we gots us some brains right here!" He slapped Jeremiah on the butt then grabbed his arm. "I thinks we gotta new slave foreman...ya ready for dat, boy?"

"Yassuh, I be ready!"

The boss pushed his lips against Jeremiah's ear than pulled back. Jeremiah could smell the fried garlic and okra stuck in his tobacco-stained teeth. The man needed a serious cleaning. Perspiration stains, some dry, others wet, marked the front of his cotton shirt. The boiling hot day conjured up body odors reminiscent of rotten cheese; his crotch smelled like a billy goat's breath. He was filthier than the slaves.

"Where ya going, boy...'fraid a me?"

Jeremiah jumped back. "No, boss, I here." He noticed the boss had a wooden leg.

"Ya stay now, boy, get dese slaves making bricks like ya showed me." With that he limped away toward the kilns. Jeremiah kept his eyes on him until he disappeared.

"Can't be taking much more dis," he whispered then clenched his fists. "Man stinks terrible bad."

A thousand times he wanted to strike out and run. A month earlier, in the midst of a numbing depression, the unexpected happened. While working in the pits, he met and befriended Messiah, a new slave from upper Louisiana. Messiah's voice and manner of speaking reminded Jeremiah of his father and brought hope back into Jeremiah's life. The Louisiana slave was unaccountably happy. The gnawing ache of melancholy in Jeremiah's belly disappeared and he regained the patience needed to plan his escape.

"My Lawd, Jeremiah, dat be a happy voice over der...mus be time for lunch," said Messiah, pointing to the left. The sound of a woman laughing turned their attention toward an open window. Jeremiah could hear the clink of silverware on china, but the angle was too high for him to see the table. The aroma of fried chicken and roasted turnips brought back bittersweet memories. Jeremiah tilted his nose up and sniffed. The scent of home cooking flowed through his nasal passages then settled on the sides of his tongue. "Smell like mama's chicken, sure nuf."

A crow squawked in the distance. Jeremiah turned toward the sound and for the first time noticed the long view toward the Yazoo and Mississippi. Rows of trees faded into the distance with the cool river waters caught in between. Far out, the hills turned violet in the summer heat and joined with the sky.

"Der," he whispered, "der I gonna be..."

One who expects nothing, enjoys everything.
SAINT FRANCIS

WATERLOO, NEW YORK - SPRING 1856

Thomas McClintock stood on the corner of Main and Virginia, leaning into the northeast wind. A late spring snow storm had buried the roads under two feet of drifts, so he came to see if his drug store could be opened.

"Hey, Billy, how's it looking?"

"Cain't tell, Mista McClintock, wind be pushing snow up dese doors."

Billy loved Waterloo. He stayed back while all the other slaves moved on to Canada, desperate to take the last step to freedom. The dangerous night voyage across Lake Ontario didn't appeal to him. He knew he risked capture but he felt at home in Waterloo.

"I don't know Billy, even if we open who's going to come out in this holy mess?"

"Maybe dey be needing some laudanum or a wool coat?" He looked at McClintock for guidance.

"Perhaps you're right," he glanced up into the heavens, "we are here to serve the Lord, our friends must be provided for, especially in such weather."

"So I be opening den?"

"Open the doors wide, my friend, God's love cannot be locked away, we are here to ease the burden of our fellow man."

Thomas, a Quaker, saw God in most everything. He came from Philadelphia in 1836, a hardened abolitionist, and along with his wife Mary, he participated in the first women's rights convention in nearby Seneca Falls. His store offered only slave-free products, some of which came from the local woolen mill owned by his landlord, Richard Hunt.

"I'm worried about you tonight, Billy."

The runaway worked for McClintock by day then disappeared into the fields at night as a guide on the underground railroad. "Ya knows Mista McClintock, there be a group of fugitives fleeing through Ithaca tonight," he said looking away to avoid eye contact. "Dey needs my help." Billy lacked confidence because of his unusual appearance. His right eye was missing. A poorly aligned glass replacement, stuck into his eye socket by a quack doctor in Chattanooga, gave his face a frightful look.

"God help you, Billy, I smell trouble." McClintock put his hand on the fugitive's shoulder hoping to change his mind.

"I be good, no worry ya self."

"Too many close calls lately, you gave us a good scare last week."

A few days before, just north of Watkins Glen, Federal Marshals surprised a family of runaways just before Billy could get to them. The husband and wife, with four young children, were manacled, beaten and dragged away. He came close to attacking the law officers but held back, he didn't want to cause problems for McClintock.

"Look at this," Thomas held up a piece of paper, "came in the mail yesterday from my friends in Philadelphia."

Billy turned the tattered paper in his hand, put it to his nose. It smelled of horse sweat. "Read it to me, Mista McClintock."

BEWARE!!

~ ~ ~

COLORED PEOPLE
OF PHILADELPHIA

~ ~ ~

AVOID CONTACT WITH POLICE OFFICERS
AND SOUTHERN AGENTS
They are empowered to act as
SLAVE CATCHERS AND KIDNAPPERS
Keep your eyes OPEN!!

~ ~ ~

"Our people, dey alway be on de run, Mister McClintock..."

"Trust no one, Billy, you hear me?" McClintock, a station master, offered his house as a refuge for runaways on the way to Canada.

It was dangerous work. McClintock faced a Federal fine of $1000 and six months hard time in prison if the marshals caught him. For Billy it would be worse. If he were lucky he would be beaten and dragged back to the plantation wearing a heavy iron slave collar covered with bells...or he might die. That was more likely since he didn't intend to return south. Most fugitives saw Canada as the promised land, but for Billy his final home was Waterloo. He loved Thomas and Mary, there could be no better place. As he saw it, he planned to live in heaven, the one in Waterloo or the one up above.

"I knows, Mista McClintock, I knows all ta well." He looked away again, but this time he reached into his pocket. "Look here," he unfolded a crumpled paper and handed it to Thomas, "what dis say?"

"My heavens, Billy, where did you get this?"

"Found it on da ground...one de Marshals drop it by mistake when dey beatin' dat po family las week near Watkins Glen."

"Can't hardly believe what I'm reading, getting to be like the big city here...don't know what to expect next."

SIX HUNDRED DOLLARS REWARD

Runaways from Edwin Jefferson, last month. A negro family of two adults and four children. Elijah Sanders, 27 years old, almost six feet tall, walks with a limp, light coffee complexion, very strong and soft spoken. He ran off with his wife, Phoebe Powers, a dark mulatto of short stature and shy affect with small pox scars across her right check and chin. Their four female children, ages 5-10, are all emaciated and sickly. I will deliver to the finder the above reward if captured in Isle of Wright County or two thirds of what they sell for if found out of the County or Virginia.

Edwin Jefferson, March 14, 1856
Printed in Isle of Wright County

"You see, Billy, the Southerns are everywhere, you must be careful."

"I lookout fur myself sure nuff, Mista McClintock."

"Not going to be easy in this weather."

"No ya worry...snow hold dem slave catchers close ta fire."

"What time you expecting to make it back here?"

"Gonna be near midnight. How I gonna git dem to ya hous...thar be footprints in snow all de way."

"I'll take the horses out for a ride along the canal, you come through there, walk in my tracks."

"I be good, you see soon nuf."

"Remember, Billy, the Lord's ways are mysterious but he watches over those who do his business."

It was time. Jeremiah had worked patiently for nine months. The masters trusted him, respected his ability to move the brick making along in an efficient manner. The courthouse project remained well ahead of schedule thanks to Jeremiah. He pleased the white masters and in return they gave him freedom at the work site.

"Here come de massa, I prayn' he make no trubble," said Messiah. Whenever his new friend spoke it lifted Jeremiah's spirit. The languid way he pronounced massa was music to Jeremiah's ears. It seemed as if his father had found a way to be present.

"How much longer," snapped the boss, "shit boy, gitcher ass moving so we's can git outta here?"

"I be quick, boss, four more loads an' we finish."

"When it's done ya take Messiah and clean up de molds down the river."

To feign respect, Jeremiah slowly moved his head up and down. The bosses liked to think they were treating him well. It was a perfect bargain for them. The foremen received a bonus for every day they moved ahead of schedule and not a penny of it went to Jeremiah. But, no matter, Jeremiah was about to change things on his own.

"Now imagine dis boy, the chief's grinnin' like a possum," purred the foreman. He adjusted his privates with a quick push across the front of his pants. "He's so happy with ya progress he's giving us Saturday off!"

"All us?"

"Everyone, even ya niggers."

"Well praise de Lawd, I thankful for dat." Messiah raised his hands toward the sky. "Dis my bless hour!"

Jeremiah waited a moment until the boss walked away then troweled a slab of clay into the mold. He wiped off the excess, smoothed the top surface just the way the masons liked it, then removed the brick from the mold and did something he had never done before. He pushed his thumb twice into the soft clay at the end of the brick and made a clear flaw. He passed it to Messiah whose job it was to inspect and trim the bricks before drying. When Messiah saw the thumb marks his eyes widened.

"Messiah, we be going to da river, dis be our time, ya hear me?"

"Yassuh, boss, yassuh." Messiah froze, too scared to move. The thumbprints were a prearranged signal to begin their escape. Jeremiah knew better than to speak of dangerous things at the worksite so they had settled on the brick flaw as a silent sign.

Messiah stared at the flaw then reached for a trowel to fix it. "I thinken I have more work to do, ya go."

"No, Messiah, we be free tonight, git to river."

"No, Jeremiah, ya go, I be fixen brick." What had been a well conceived escape plan now seemed flawed and dangerous to Messiah, he smelled trouble in the air.

"Ya done, Messiah, give it here." He took the brick and placed it on the drying rack.

"Let me fix it."

"No, ya go."

"I love ya, boss, but I be stayin'." Messiah imagined dogs chasing him down, tearing his flesh, ripping out his neck. It made no sense, he was happy making bricks.

"We mus' follow boss orders." Jeremiah grabbed him hard by the arm. "Ya no be disappointing me now, it be time...I see da light...our day be here."

"Hey, boys, ya skedaddlin'?" The spray of the foreman's saliva hit Messiah square in the face, "I told ya once, git ya ass that away, down thar to the river. Ya boys pissin' me off now aint ya!"

Messiah wiped his face with a muddy rag, picked up a mold box and headed for the river.

Jeremiah looked back at the brick. The thumbprints were too easy to see. "Damn, I forgit something!" He turned and doubled back. When no one could see, he rotated the flawed side of the brick out of view.

"Don't need no callin' 'tention to ourselves," he whispered, then caught up with Messiah.

The soul's dark cottage, batter'd and decay'd
Lets in new light through chinks that time has made;
Stronger by weakness, wiser men become,
As they draw near to their eternal home.
Leaving the old, both worlds at once they view,
That stand upon the threshold of the new.

EDMUND WALLER

Delaware River - Fall 1863

The broad oceanlike expanse of Delaware Bay was far behind now. In the face of the receding tide, the frigate slowed as eddies and swirling rips pounded the bow and pushed the ship around. New Jersey loomed on the right, a few hundred yards away. Off to the left, the Delaware shore drew closer.

The fragrant smell of the piney forests along the banks brought back memories of the plantation. Jeremiah could hardly remember a time when life was settled, but the year before his mother was sold held a few good memories. Hany had worked hard to fill the empty space after her husband's death. She focused her love on cooking. On Sundays she walked through the fields to buy a side of bacon, then fixed a breakfast of boiled corn and biscuits to go with the crackling meat. For dessert there might be some flitch and fried corn cake, or on special days, flannel cakes. He could still smell the sweet perfume of butter mixed with sugar and vanilla.

Most nights after everyone was in bed his mother told tales of Africa. Jeremiah's favorite was about a lost lion cub her grandfather had saved from the village dogs. The cub slept with the children and ate on the table with the family. Hany set a plate for the cub near her chair. The little lion always wagged his tail in her rice knocking it in all directions. The adults at the table would scream at the little lion who would then roll on his back and purr. One day he rolled a little too far and fell off the table sending Hany's plate to the floor with him. Fortunately, it was a wooden plate, but the commotion scared the cub so much he did two flips and ran away. Jeremiah always slept peacefully after hearing his mother tell the tale.

"Sergeant, we'll be putting into New Castle in about half an hour, get your men ready."

"Yassuh, Captain, I movin' now." Jeremiah's mind raced as his thoughts drifted back to the plantation. He could hear the rattled breathing of the filthy planter who bought his mother as mere chattel, her eyes full of fear when he forced her mouth open to look for rotten teeth. Jeremiah could still feel the dried salt on his checks from the tears that flowed on the day his mother was manacled and taken away. He had run to stop the wagon, to break her chains. He never saw the fist that brought him down as she reached out to touch him. When he regained consciousness she was gone.

"You OK, Sergeant?"

"I be fine when we git off dis ship." Jeremiah saluted the ensign then walked toward the aft deck to secure his baggage. His army issue hobnail boots never felt right and less so on the slick boards of the frigate. He reached into his pocket for a cloth to wipe his face but found a folded newspaper clipping instead. The yellowed paper was all that remained of his parent's possessions. His father had torn the advertisement out of a newspaper just after he sailed into Charleston on the slave ship *Evening Star*. When he docked he found the newspaper, with the advertisement circled in brown ink, cast on the deck. He would have been punished if he had been caught with the paper but he took the risk to save some trace of his past.

** WINDWARD COAST SLAVES. - *The sale of the frigate* Aphrodite's *Cargo of prime Windward Coast SLAVES will commence THIS DAY, the 26th inst. at 11 o'clock at Gadsden's Wharf. Apply to*

thursday may 26. 1814   *M. CHRISTIAN*

** THE SALES OF THE SHIP DEMETER'S *Cargo of 225 PRIME NEGROES, from* Bonny, *to be held on board THIS DAY at Gadsden's Wharf.*

wednesday may 25. 1814   *CHARLES FISH*

The swaying motion of the ship sloshed his lunch around the walls of his stomach and back up his throat. He tried to force the reflux down with two swallows but it kept rising.

"Private Bear, git your gear together." Jeremiah reached down to help him with his haversack and felt the first wave of nausea. *Been on this ship too long,* he thought, *time to get back on steady ground.*

"Sergeant, think dat's where we be going?" The private pointed to an island in the middle of the river a mile aft. "Secesh be waiting der, Sarge?"

"We be finding out soon nuf, Private Bear." Jeremiah hacked up a ball of phlegm and spat it over the side. "Can't imagine it," he lied, "look like just marsh and birds ta me."

The private met up with Jeremiah in Baltimore when they boarded the frigate. Bear wasn't his real name, but everyone called him that after he told the group about the day he wrestled a bear in the Tennessee woods. The name stuck, not because anyone believed the story, but because they thought he was just a happy fool making up tall tales.

"It be an island we go ta, Sarge?"

"It be so." Jeremiah wanted to explain to Bear and the rest of the detachment where they were going but his orders forbade disclosure of the details. The soldiers, all former slaves eager to confront the rebels, would not have been pleased to know their destination. The colonel trusted only Jeremiah and the lieutenant with the truth. Surely, some of them would have deserted if they knew how many Confederates they would face and under what circumstances.

"Ya be a little green der, Sarge."

The dance of the ship in the churning river had begun to make him dizzy, his stomach lost its balance, his hands turned greasy and cold.

"Can't be believing but I gettin' seasick."

The fetid odor of bilge wash, mixed in with the smell of boiled cabbage from the galley, overwhelmed the sergeant. He rushed to grab hold of the rail and vomited over the side into the green river wash. He stayed there, face down, hanging out over the rush of the Delaware waters and imagined how good the cold water would feel on his sweaty face. His mind went blank for a moment then slipped back to the first night on the run outside Vicksburg.

Adrift in the middle of the Yazoo River, Jeremiah was in trouble. Messiah, a full four inches taller, had an advantage, his head cleared the river surface. Jeremiah, bounced up and down on extended toes, barely touching bottom each time his nose went underwater.

"If dis git deeper I finish Messiah."

"Come here, boss, sand bar over der."

The lights of Vicksburg flickered in the distance. Over to the left a fishing skiff glided down river in the gathering mist.

"Help me up."

"You gonna make it, boss, grab on, it shallow here."

The slaves had done the only thing that made sense, they jumped into the river and swam to the middle. Horses, dogs and gunners would be coming soon. The common wisdom for fugitives was to move at night through water to cover their tracks.

"I skeered, boss, dis water's cold, makin' me shake bad."

"Over der."

"Where?"

"Der, look, da sandbar by shore."

"Yasuh, boss, praise de Lawd, we be saved."

"Oh damn!"

"What, boss, ya hurt?"

"No, awww! Help me...crawdaddy git da toe!"

"Raise ya foot, I eat em right here."

"Ya makin' fun me."

"No, boss, I hungry, crawdads be my favorite food, y'all love how mah Mammy cook 'em real sweet."

Jeremiah looked into Messiah's eyes. He wanted to laugh but fear seized his jaw.

"Come dis way, look, we almost ta shore."

The current pushed them south toward the shallows on the east side of the river. A slimy boulder hidden below the surface sliced into Jeremiah's knee. He stood up in two feet of water, then waded in and collapsed on the shore. Blood dripped into the sand from his torn knee. Off to the west, heat lightning danced on the horizon.

"Dat nuf water, boss, I take my chances on land." Messiah spat out a gusher of muddy water. "I ain't no gator and da Lor knows you be worse."

Jeremiah looked down at his knee. Blood started to clot in the ragged wound. "Ya right Messiah, water be trouble, sooner face da bounty hunters on land."

"Yassuh, boss, jus be calm now, git ya breath back."

"We gotta move, dis be no place ta rest," Jeremiah turned around, "look der, we only few miles below the city." Fishing lights bobbed on the far side of the river, distant voices mixed with laughter. Just ahead the forest floor glowed white in the fading moonlight. The pungent turpentine scent of scrub pine mixed in with the rotten fish smell of the sandy bottoms.

"Der, we need to move dat way, gotta be way far 'fore light."

Messiah's face broke into a big smile. "I with ya boss, we go south, down Mississippi, back ta my place."

Jeremiah could almost taste the food that would come from the kitchen of Messiah's Louisiana home.

"What, boss, what ya thinkin'?"

"I have no home, you neither now."

"No, ya be home with me, my mama keep us safe."

"Too dangerous, Messiah, we be fugitives now, mus' go north ta freedom."

"Dat lot a walkin' boss, Louisiana whole lot closer, I promist."

"Shh! Listen, ya hear somethin'?"

The hairs stood up on Jeremiah's neck, he sensed a change in the air. The night breeze smelled of honeysuckle, mixed now with a foul animal scent that reminded him of the swine pens back home.

"Must be farm..."

"Boss look der... light!"

"Shh!"

In an instant their world turned. The slaves had stumbled into a bunch of coon hunters working the banks.

"Hey, Jessie what de heck spookin' dem dogs?"

"What the fuck, Ben...dogs musta found a fox den thataway!"

"Son a bitch, I ner seen no fox up a tree!"

The hunters had no idea who was there but the hounds went right to Messiah. He scrambled to climb higher. The first dog, a female, clamped his ankle in her mouth and held on until the big hounds arrived. Jeremiah changed his mind fast, all of a sudden the river seemed like the safest place in Mississippi. He held his breath and backed into the water.

"Shit, Jessie, lookie here, I 'spect it be the tallest fox I ever seen!"

"Reckon we got dinner?"

"Hell no, we gots us a big tar baby."

"What you mean...oh shit, what's he doing here?"

"Here, nigger boy, lookie here, where ya from?"

"Louisiana, massa, I be from down da river."

"Louisiana, shit boy, you need a whuppin'...y'all lying now ain't ya?"

"No boss, help me!"

"Help ya shit, maybe a shot up de ass will loosen ya tongue!"

Jeremiah drifted a hundred yards out, far enough to let the current take him. He spread his arms on the surface and settled into the water. From the shore all that could be seen was the faint silhouette of his head. A moment later he disappeared.

New Castle, Delaware - Fall 1863

Jeremiah could have sworn he had just landed in tidewater Virginia. The small port looked more like a Southern town than the Pennsylvania and New York villages he knew. The brick colonial houses and churches had the old English look he associated with his year up and down the Rappahannock. One of the sailors had told Jeremiah that New Castle was originally a Dutch town, that someone named William Penn landed there in 1682, but it meant nothing to him.

"Get your men formed up, Sergeant." The lieutenant gestured from across the street toward the town square. His erect and robust stature fit the image of a Union officer. He had his mens' full respect, not because of his appearance but because of the danger he had assumed as their commander. The Rebel government made it clear that any Union officer captured with black troops would meet the same fate as his men: immediate execution.

"Yassuh, Lieutenant, we be ready to eat." Jeremiah loved the Army. It gave him a path up, out of the world of slavery. Since the day he put on his Union Blues he spoke with enthusiasm to his leaders. The uniform hung well on his lean six foot frame. His cropped hair and handsome mouth set him apart, he looked like a warrior. Most of the white soldiers, with their greasy long locks and ragged beards, seemed scraggy in comparison. His positive attitude and sharp appearance was noticed and he made sergeant during his first year of enlistment.

But there was something else that set him apart. He was one of the few men of the United States Colored Troops who wore the Medal of Honor. A year earlier, in the midst of battle, he rescued a major. He raced into a melee and fought hand to hand with five rebels to free his white commander, then he dragged two of the men back as prisoners. Jeremiah didn't talk much about it, the medal was enough.

"The packet boat should be here about 1300, that'll give ya time to get some food," said the lieutenant. "Report to the river dock area after you eat."

"Where da mess, Lieutenant?"

"None here, Sergeant, try the tavern, just past the courthouse, over there...relax a little."

Jeremiah noticed the lieutenant's improved mood. "Ya happy to be off the water, sir?"

"Damn ship makin' me sick," he replied, "feelin' much better now, thank you...now move on, Sergeant, the men look hungry."

The sergeant pointed toward a two story brick row house with green double hung windows. A red signboard hung over the front door with the words *Smith's Alehouse* in gold leaf letters and a painting of a schooner flanked by two large anchors. The air smelled of mildew and rotten meat.

"Damn, Sarge, dis here town smell terrible bad, like de back end of a sick Reb!"

Jeremiah motioned around the corner. "Look down da alley, Private."

The private came running back waving both hands, "You right 'bout dat Sarge, damn cat caught in a broke cellar window, rottin' like a bad apple."

"Nothin' to be done 'bout dat...It's noon and ya hear da lieutenant," he said, pointing toward the alehouse. "We no eatin' military food ta day."

"Ya drink da ale, Sarge?" said Bear.

"Never seen it an' neither will you dis day."

"Some kinda barley drink with bubbles, dats what I be told."

"Don't sound no good."

The black detachment, still a little wobbly from the sea voyage, made their way down the cobblestone street toward the tavern. Two local girls, stared at them, mouths agape.

"Locals don't look friendly, Sarge."

"Don't pay no mind...thank da Lawd, we be leaving dis town soon nuf." Nothing in New Castle felt good to Jeremiah. He still feared a slave catcher would show up and arrest his men.

"Dey be missing flag." The corporal stood before the tavern door under an empty pole attached to the second floor wall. Jeremiah looked around and saw the flags had been removed from all but one of the poles in town. Only the courthouse had the new 35-star Union banner. He remembered the 34 star flag. It was the one he saluted when he joined the Army in 1862. The thirty-fifth star came in June of 1863 when West Virginia split off from Virginia.

"Open da door, Corporal, we not here to inspect flag poles."

"Stan' back," shouted Private Bear, "let me in first, I be starvin'!" He crossed the threshold and found himself in a room full of white men sitting in a cloud of blue tobacco smoke. Jeremiah came in behind Bear and stopped just short of knocking him over. The customers stared, surprised that a group of slaves in Union blue had invaded their tavern. The room went silent, the only sound the creaking of the wooden plank floor as the soldiers shifted their weight against the oily boards. Two sputtering tallow candles and a model ship sat on the fireplace mantle.

"We be here for lunch." There was no reply. The smells and colors of the interior left little to the imagination. Scattered in the room were seven greasy oak tables, each with a group of sullen men, sticky ale mugs in hand. The room smelled of stale beer, burnt meat, boiled beans and rancid mutton fat. Moldy mustard-colored plaster walls glowed in the smoky light of the brass wall sconces.

"Lunch, we here ta eat." Jeremiah repeated. "Ya hear me, who be in charge here." He felt pressure building in his forehead, his eyes went out of focus. "Dis a shit hole," he whispered. Dirty dishes with old rib bones smeared in gravy sat on a sideboard to his right. Mouse droppings fouled the floor.

"What ya say boy...we'un's no be needing more darkies..." said a grizzled man with a checkered muslin shirt. He wiped his mouth with both his sleeves and pointed his fork at Jeremiah.

"Now jus a minute, Jessie, you be quiet now," came a voice from the bar, "dese men be here to help us."

"Help us, fuck that shit..."

Jeremiah turned left to find the speaker but his eye settled on a tattered Rebel battle flag hanging from a beam near the bar. At first he thought it was soiled but then he realized there were bullet holes in the red field between the stars and bars.

"What can we do for ya men?" The barkeeper was a large man and the words rolled off his tongue like he expected no reply. His face was red from drink, he looked like trouble. Jeremiah remembered his mother's voice telling the story of the parting of the Red Sea, how it swallowed up evil.

"Food, sir," began Bear, "been sent to eat...Lawd knows we needs supper."

"Land's sakes, boy, ain't nothin' here to eat!" The man threw his bar rag into the sink and started to approach the soldiers.

"No boy here," said Jeremiah.

"What'd you say...ain't no call..."

"You call me Sergeant...I not ya boy."

"You rag-tag son a bitch..." The man's face shifted toward purple.

"Son a bitch, Jake, that black boy corrected ya good now, didn't he?"

"I said no food boy...what's the problem, ya got a corncob stuck up ya ass?"

The door opened and in walked the lieutenant. "What's going on?"

"Man says no food for us."

The lieutenant looked confused, he had just had lunch there an hour earlier. A quick glance around the room gave him his answer. "I'll be sure to tell the quartermaster about your hospitality...you've seen the last of Army business here."

"But, Lieutenant, sir, it's jus' these boys..."

"We're finished here." The lieutenant had heard rumors of such behavior in Delaware and Maryland but he had never seen it. "The packet boat has arrived men, form up outside."

Jeremiah started to leave then turned back toward the barkeep. "Open ya windows, smell like garbage here," he said then waited a moment, "it not da food."

"The shore's straight ahead, 'bout a hundred yards."

"Can't feel da bottom," whispered Jeremiah, "water be terrible cold." It had been four months on the run and here he was again, floating in dark waters late at night.

The old captain laughed then backed his skiff away. "Ain't no bottom here son, water's 500 feet deep...right up to shore."

"Ya not leavin' me, boss...cain't swim!"

"Just hold that board I gave ya, kick them feet like heck."

"Take me closer."

"Can't son, too many marshals out." He tipped his hat, as if that would help. "Head toward that light like I told ya...nothing to it."

The man pulled hard on the oars. "Ask for Billy...he's your man."

Jeremiah turned back but the boat had faded into the dark. For a few minutes Jeremiah could hear the rattling of the oarlocks, then silence. He started to panic at the thought of the distance to the lake bottom, tried not to think how long it would take for a body to sink that far. "Sweet Jesus," he shouted. "Mah lawd, jus hold me up...I be good...I knows I be good!" He turned and headed toward shore, his hands tight on the slick board, his feet kicking like a man trying to save himself.

"Hey, who der?"

"Jus' me."

"Jus' me, who dat?" said Jeremiah. He started to swim back out, away from shore.

"Where ya going, boy, dis here's where ya belong." The stranger lifted a lantern to show a slick black face. "Here grab dis rope."

Jeremiah released the board and let the rope pull him in. "Don't pull so hard, mah hands be numb."

"Git ya ass up here, we gotta move."

"Ya Billy?"

"Dat's me...youse got a pack a questions don't ya now!" Billy extended a muscular arm and pulled Jeremiah up out of the dark water.

The scent of musty grapes hung in the air.

"I be Jeremiah, been to..." He stopped, Billy was right in his face. A stream of green pus oozed out of the left corner of the stranger's right eye and ran down the side his nose. There was no iris, just a white glass ball stuck into the eye socket.

"What's got inta ya, friend?"

"Sorry, Billy, ya eye, it..."

"Ya be forgiving me now..." Billy stepped back and felt his glass eye, then pulled a soiled handkerchief out of his pocket and rotated the glass until he felt the raised pigment of the iris. When he turned back to face Jeremiah, the painted blue iris was in place, although a bit off center.

Jeremiah felt faint. He reached out for Billy's arm to steady himself, "I not so good...but least I outta dat lake."

"Ya be better now." He handed Jeremiah a burlap sack. "Git dat wet stuff off...here some dry clothes." Jeremiah started to turn away. "Look at me boy, where ya from?"

"Vicksburg...Maryland 'for dat."

"Damn, nigger, ya wet clothes smell like donkey shit...throw em in da lake."

"What ya expect?" began Jeremiah, then he decided to hold his tongue. It had been a hard trip with many nights spent on the foul floors of goat and sheep sheds. He wasn't sure what goat cheese tasted like, but if it was anything like the smell of their breath he would never go near the stuff.

"See dem torches moving on da ridge?"

"Dey ya friends, I pray ta Jesus?"

"Dem's slave catchers up from Maryland...jus' arrived dis week!"

Jeremiah rubbed the water from his eyes and squinted, but all he could make out was the dark shadow of a horse in the distance. He just wanted to sleep.

"Over der, gotta move," said Billy. "Behind dat rock be a cave."

"Not dis slave...we be trapped in der." Jeremiah raised his hands and moved back. "I knows I safer in da lake."

"Hear dat, Jeremiah?" The choppy bark of a hound echoed off the distant ridge. "Git ya ass in da cave or we be finish."

Jeremiah looked at Billy, tried to figure if he knew his business. For the first time he took in his size. Jeremiah stood six feet, but Billy was taller with thick arms and legs. If he was going against Billy there would be no talking, he'd just have to turn and run. Billy understood as much. In one swift motion he grabbed Jeremiah's arm and dragged him to the cave.

"What da hell, Billy!" It was pitch dark in the cave and he tripped going in.

"Watcha step, Jeremiah, der's more'n you here."

He knelt down and brushed against something fleshy. "Jesus is my Lawd!"

"Shush ya self!"

"Who der?" He saw people gathered in small groups on the floor. One family had three children, another a young boy and a baby. "Dis some kinda hideout, what dey doin' here?"

"Waitin' like you for da way ta Waterloo."

"Waterloo, whar dat?"

"Village at the north end of da lake...last stop before ya cross ta Canada."

"What dat, shhh!" The clip clop of horses passing nearby echoed through the cave. "Shoulda jumped back in dat lake," he whispered, "we cooked."

Jeremiah crawled back toward the entrance to see better. Two men stood off to the right about a hundred yards away, their mounts grazing along the tree line.

Billy tiptoed over to the family with the baby. "Ya babe's stirring, cain't afford no noise, give em some dis." He handed the mother a small flacon of laudanum. She dipped her pinky into the reddish-brown liquid, tasted it, then drew it slowly across the child's lips. The baby coughed twice and buried his head in the woman's breast. The mother spit the bitter liquid into a cotton rag, then felt around in her bag, pulled out a brown egg and peeled the shell using her free hand.

Billy turned back toward Jeremiah. "Speak...what on ya mind?" Jeremiah moved his head as if to say no, then began fidgeting with his top shirt button.

"Get back here!" called out Billy. Jeremiah had launched himself back into the night. He made it halfway across the clearing before the riders saw him trip and fall. He stayed down, praying the men would miss him in the dark.

"Git ya black ass up, boy!" Jeremiah stayed face down, doing his best to imitate a dark rock. "Ya heard me, move it, boy!"

Can't be, thought Jeremiah, *no way they found me.* He felt a sharp stone under his elbow and grabbed it with his fist.

"Shoot his ass, Jake."

"Fuck, what'cha doing on the ground der nigger boy?"

"Git up, ya bastard, I whup ya good upside ya haid!"

"Stand back, I gives him a good lickin'."

"Shit no, let's see if dis steel blade gits him moving!"

Jeremiah opened one eye and saw the flash of a knife in the moonlight. In an instant he thrust the stone deep into the temple of the nearest slave catcher. The damage was so bad that the other two riders froze long enough for Jeremiah to bolt between their horses. As he passed he dug his fingernails into the flesh of the animals' haunches. One rider fell off his bucking mount and cracked his head on a boulder. The other tried to control his horse, but the gray stallion bolted toward the tree line and flung the rider into a white oak, impaling him on a broken branch.

The Confederate lieutenant could not believe his luck. He joined the 3rd Mississippi Volunteers to kill Yankees and here he sat, assigned to guard the courthouse district while all the action was down along the river. The rail thin officer had an abiding hatred for the northern aggressors encircling Vicksburg. He knew that killing blue coats, and lots of them, was the only way to free Vicksburg, but killing time was about all he'd experienced since the battle began on May 19.

"Listen, sir, Union guns startin' up agin." The first sergeant cupped his chaffed ears and pointed west.

"Rekun the bastards will concentrate on the ramparts, ain't nothing here gonna help 'em." The lieutenant was a redhead with a fiery temperament. He motioned toward the empty stores, homes and civic buildings around the square. "We should be down along the river whupping the tar otta them Yanks!"

"Nuttin' to be done 'bout it, sir." The first sergeant stroked his beard. He didn't like seeing his lieutenant upset. "Itsa mighty purty courthouse, Lieutenant, look at all that spittin' new brick."

"Dawg gone shame, Sergeant, hardly finished it before the Yanks started marching south. Ya got to admire what they built here, a courthouse as handsome as can be with all them porticoes and Ionic columns." The lieutenant had just started college when the war began, hoping to learn enough to start an architecture practice, but all he remembered were the three classic orders.

"Sure sits up here nice and peaceful on top of the hill and all."

"'Spect it have been prettier with Corinthian columns." The lieutenant looked away toward the river. "Never been a fan of the Ionic, looks too womanly."

"Ya got me on that one, Lieutenant."

"Never mind, it be..."

"Get down sir, stray shell comin'..." He grabbed the officer's sleeve and pulled him behind a large oak trunk.

"Dadgum, Sergeant, that was close, but..."

"Maybe we gonna see some action yet."

"Why they shooting up here anyhow?"

"Can't figure dem Yanks."

"They jus' wasting powder. All they got ta do is starve us out. The son a bitching blockade's so tight I hear folks be eating rats for dinner an' old shoes for dessert." He turned his head and spat on the tree trunk. "Why half the town's livin' in caves."

"Here come another, sir...I do believe the Yank's are targeting the courthouse." They both looked up. "Look...to the left, ya can see it coming."

"I'll be damned, looks like it's jus' hanging in the sky now don't it?" They both knew the biggest Union guns were mounted on ships which forced the naval gunners to send their shells on a high trajectory. It was basic physics, a level shot would hardly make the shoreline, so the gun angles were ratcheted up until they were close to vertical. It was like mortar fire, pretty much straight up and straight down, and quite visible if you knew where to look.

"Son a bitch, that shell's gonna drop right on the courthouse."

"No more Ionic columns...whoa, lookie here!" The round landed in the courthouse square exploding the pavement and the statue of a Mexican War general. "Good shot, they got dem a bronze Reb! No need ta call a doctor."

The air was heavy with brick dust and the acrid smell of gunpowder. The lieutenant drew the aroma of burning sulphur and saltpeter up high into his nose and held it like good tobacco smoke. He loved the smell, it reminded him of his hunting rifle. For a moment he imagined he was back home in the scrub woods standing in a cloud of smoke watching a three point buck thrash on the ground.

"Ain't nothing to be done, Sergeant, can't stop them damn river guns from up here." He turned and kicked a loose stone in the direction of the Union ships. "For God's sake, man, if I gets the chance I'm gonna tell General Pemberton himself there's no damn need for us sitting like lumps on this stupid hill...I'd fight 'em alone, ya know that."

"Preshate ya desire to git into the fight, sir. We be useless as dead cats up here…" he said, then pushed his hand into his pocket. "Taste this, sir." He pulled out a paper packet and unwrapped it to reveal a shining hunk of skilly golee.

"You shitting me, Sergeant!"

"No, try it, fried it myself, soaked the hard tack for a good hour."

"That's trash."

"Sir, pardon me…my ma sent me a ball of her best pork fat. I browned the biscuit in it, even found some salt."

"You sure 'bout this? I'll spit it on your boot if it tastes half as bad as it looks."

The first sergeant straightened up and puffed out his chest. "Look here, it's just like ma makes at home…ya gonna like it." He held out the greasy morsel and the commander took it between his thumb and forefinger, holding it like a dead rodent. He lifted it to eye level, sniffed it once, then took a tiny bite.

"Jesus Lordy, it's a motherfucker!" He chewed harder to push out the flavor, worked it against the roof of his mouth. "Damn fine, Sergeant…'spect I taste some hickory smoke in there…ya send my regards to mama!"

The shock of the unexpected pleasure of the greasy morsel jolted his senses, sent him into a trance. He looked up, first at the sergeant, then over his shoulder toward the river. In the distance he could make out the far side of the water, a warm green under the midday sun. Shades of gray, purple and red mixed in the vapors along the horizon. For an instant he wondered how killing could exist alongside a taste as divine as the skilly golee.

"Sir, ya alright?"

"No, it's…"

"What, Lieutenant?" There was no time for a reply. The sergeant followed the lieutenant's eyes to the top of the courthouse where a shell was dropping neatly through the cupola, piercing the heart of the building. A sucking sound filled the air. The round sliced deep into the courthouse, followed by an explosion. Brick and glass flew in all directions, mixing into a lethal maelstrom of grit and dust. The first sergeant reacted too late. Through the fog of debris a single brick flew straight and true into his chest like a comet from the heavens. One moment he was there, moving toward cover behind a cast iron fence and then he was nothing but a mist of blood, flesh and bone shard.

"Sergeant?" The lieutenant, focused on the explosion, had no idea what happened behind him. He reached back for the sergeant while keeping his eye on the courthouse. His hand brushed against a brick lodged between the pointed metal spikes of the fence. It was still warm from the explosion, smoking but intact after its swift flight from the cupola. He leaned down, set his boot against the fencepost and dislodged it.

"Sergeant, look at this shit?" He held out the brick to show his comrade. "There's thumbprints pressed into the end, now who would have done such a thing?"

In the cloud of dust the lieutenant could hardly see three feet ahead. "Sergeant, where the hell are ya?"

Billy pushed and pulled the runaways along. "Jus a bit more...we be home den." The ragged group working their way down the canal tow path looked all wrong. The women, with babies hidden in their aprons, were agitated, out of place.

"Billy, why we not be hidin' til dark?"

"It be right, dis my town." Billy tried to sound calm but panic glazed his eyes. He had never brought runaways into town during daylight.

"Cain't be good no how to walk in like dis," said Jeremiah. "For Lor's sake we gots us three dead lawmen on our hands." His usual escape into the saving waters was not an option; jumping into a canal wouldn't get him much.

"We mus' move faster." Billy grabbed the hand of one of the boys and pulled him. "Keep de pace!"

"I neber walked in no town in daylight since I left Vicksburg," Jeremiah repeated, then stopped dead in his tracks. "Dat's nuf a dis, I knows all hell 'bout ta break loose."

"Move long, Jeremiah..."

"I be staying here, looka de people up der," he said, then turned back. "Am I dreamin'...sure nuf dats da law."

Billy grabbed his arm and gave him a sharp slap on the cheek. "Ya get ya ass up front 'fore we be kilt." He pointed toward the town marshal standing under an oak tree by the Washington Street bridge. "Head for dat bridge."

"Not me boss." Everything in Jeremiah's being was telling him to defy Billy, to save himself.

"Git yourself over der!"

"No, dat a lawman." Jeremiah stopped again and Billy gave him a kick. The rest of the slaves were wide-eyed, sure that Jeremiah had it right.

"Damn, Billy," called out the marshal, "where the hell you been!"

"We be thro' de trubbles…"

"You have no idea…get these folks right quick into the basement of the Eagle Hotel."

"Yassa," Billy began, "but Jeremiah here…"

"Get moving, we'll talk later."

"Lord knows, we been mighty worried about you Billy," whispered Ben McClintock. Ben was the son of Thomas McClintock. He had taken Billy under his protection after his father left Waterloo for Philadelphia. He formed the slaves in a line to move them along faster, then pulled Billy to the rear.

"Once we get this group hidden in the Eagle you come to my house with Jeremiah."

"Jeremiah's…" mumbled Billy.

"Not now, Billy." Ben patted him on the shoulder and ran back to the front to help the marshal."

"I'll get them settled Ben, you go home with Billy and Jeremiah," the marshal said, a chaw of tobacco in his left cheek. The fugitives stared. After weeks of flight from the slave catchers it was hard to believe that a lawman would help them.

"We have room at the McClintock House for three more, Marshal."

"No, you have enough trouble on your hands with those two." The lawman tipped his hat toward Ben then disappeared into the Eagle Hotel. It started to rain, a little drizzle at first, then the humidity spiked and made everyone more edgy.

"Come on, Billy, you look mighty tired, let's get you two some food."

Billy heard none of it. His face covered in sweat, his palms slippery with fear, he drew in his breath, focused on what he had to say. "Ben listen ta me… Jeremiah…he kilt dem bounty hunters las' night."

"I know, Billy, that's why you'll both be leaving tonight."

"No, massa…Waterloo…dis be my home…please massa…"

"No more, Billy, the Federals are coming in the morning, you must save yourself and Jeremiah."

Billy could hardly speak, couldn't understand. He reached out and grabbed Ben's arm. "Where, massa…where…Lor knows I done nothin' to be punish like dis."

"Easy, Billy," he whispered, pushing the front door open with his free hand. "It's too dangerous for you here." He turned toward Jeremiah. "Come in, welcome to my house."

"Mista Ben, I be happy for your kindness." Jeremiah clicked the door shut and backed up to the wall. He hadn't been in a proper home since he left the plantation. A savory aroma filled the room. The complex scents of sauteed onions, roast pork with a hint of rosemary, and the perfume of citrus furniture polish were hard to parse but his brain lit up.

"Taste this, Jeremiah." Ben handed him a biscuit slathered with butter.

"Amen, Mista Ben, I thinks I be famish!" The heavenly flavor washed away the aching fears of his journey. He placed one hand on his stomach, the other over his eyes and bowed slightly. "I be thanking ya, sir."

The sound of piano music drifted down from upstairs. It was a simple waltz but it held everyone in place. Jeremiah closed his eyes. The melody, the smells, the look of the place settled him. He could easily have fallen asleep except for a rustling sound that came from down the hall. He leaned forward for a better look. A small black woman sat on a bench reading a newspaper, her back against the wall.

"Mista Ben," she winked, "look like Congress be tired of ya anti-slavery petitions, why it say here dat some Senators be callin' Waterloo a station on de underground rail."

Ben squeezed his eyes shut, then broke into a smile. "Ain't seen no underground railroad tracks here, Harriet."

She started to chuckle then put down the paper.

"Look like ya have two fine men here, I amagine dese de boys causing da troubles."

"Well, I suspect you have that right."

Jeremiah took a closer look. She wore a navy blue wool jacket, a floor length black and white striped muslin skirt and a white cotton scarf pulled tight around the top of her head. A clean white apron hung below the jacket. Her face was round with a broad nose and piercing eyes, one more open than the other. But, what struck him the most, was the way she held her large powerful hands. Folded firmly on her stomach, they belonged to a person of determination and cunning.

"Billy, Jeremiah, this is Harriet...Harriet Tubman, she's leaving with a group tonight, best conductor in the business. She'll take you to Pulteneyville on Lake Ontario."

Jeremiah could not believe his eyes. Like most runaways he had heard of her. For the past ten years she had been leading slaves, hundreds of them, out of Maryland, her exploits so daring and effective that she carried a $50,000 bounty on her head. Among the slaves she was called Moses.

"Miss Harriet..." he began.

"Yassa?" she replied and then he knew he had heard the voice before. She had visited the plantation not long before his mother was sold. A few years later she came back with a plan for him to escape, but it was too dangerous to leave.

"Ya knew my mother."

She sat back, squinted her eyes and took a good look at Jeremiah, then stood up. "Where, son?"

"Mary's Land."

"It be a long time an' many trips..."

"We's on de Perry Town Plantation, you be der twice."

"Whut ya mama's name?"

"Hany."

Harriet's eyes shut then popped open. "Hany, yes, I thinks I remember. She a beautiful woman, strong an' ready for freedom. I be disappointed when I returned an' learned she sold. Ya ever heard a her again?" Jeremiah looked down, couldn't speak.

"I sorry, it be difficult. Now ya hear me, Jeremiah, I be a poor soul, but dis nigger know der's a war coming and we be saved. Dem white folks in de South all skeered after Johnny Brown...I orter know." She stood up, raised her hands toward the ceiling. "De Lord's gonna bring us thro de trubbles and ya see Hany on de day ob judgment." Harriet pulled Jeremiah toward her. "I seen de wust tings but de Lord be saving ya young men, be setting de niggers free, dat's a fact."

Jeremiah did something he'd never done before, he kissed a stranger on the cheek. She was not a pretty woman but there was a beauty in her that went beyond appearance. The kiss startled her, but it was all he could do, there were no words in his mouth.

"Praise de Lord, ya day come soon Jeremiah," she backed away and sat down, "now, no more dat, we mus' go."

"Yes, ma'am."

"Don't ma'am me son!" She reached down into her haversack and pulled out a small cloth bag. "Here, ya be needing dis." She placed it on a side table and untied the drawstring.

"What dis?" He spread the brown velvet open to reveal a dented metal cup, "Lord bless ya, Miss Harriet!"

Jeremiah had never met such a slave, he needed to know more.

"How ya come ta dis place?"

Harriet's eyes teared up. "Oh my, young man, too many stories ta tell. I be back to Maryland more'n ten times, brought out hundred of slaves, but da law on me now...big price on my head." She smiled for a moment, then opened her hands and grabbed Jeremiah by the shoulders. "Imagine what de Lord has done. A senator took me an' my niece ta his home...Senator Seward in Auburn just down de road." She put her hands together and raised them up. "I only be doing trips between here an' Canada now, soon I go north myself...but I be back...we find da promist land!"

Ben walked over to a roll top desk and rummaged in the top drawer for a moment. "Jeremiah," he said, "what year were you born?"

"Eighteen and thirty-five, first day da year."

Ben found what he was looking for, a leather pouch full of coins. "I'm sure the right one is here somewhere." He poured the coins onto the desk and sorted through them. "Yes, you're in luck, here's a 1935 Half Eagle and a brand new Double Eagle to go with it." He walked over and placed the heavy gold coins in Jeremiah's hand, then closed his fingers over it. "You'll be needing some money, I wish it were more." He took out four more coins and handed them to Billy then kissed him on the forehead.

Jeremiah had never received anything of value, didn't know what to make of such generosity. He looked down then up into Ben's face. "God bless ya and...." A loud banging turned all eyes toward the front door. Jeremiah took a step back.

"Hey, in there, let's git a move on!"

"You no be skeered, Mista Jeremiah, spose dats my assistant, Johnny." Harriet gave Ben a hug, picked up a tarred haversack and pointed Billy and Jeremiah toward the door. "We be coming, Johnny."

The autumn sun cut through a break in the clouds warming the back of Jeremiah's neck. By military standards the packet boat was small, in fact, if the postman hadn't given Jeremiah his seat he would have had to stand. His nose started to sting and he slapped at it. A spot of blood and a half squished mosquito danced on the end of his forefinger. He wiped it across the sloop's mast then reached for a hankie in his coat pocket and rubbed his finger.

"Lotta mail ya have der," said Bear, running his hand over one of the large canvas mail bags.

"Lots of people sending mail," snapped the postman, clearly not accustomed to talking to passengers, especially black ones.

Bear looked into the postman's face, certain he was the brother of a miller he wished he had never met in Maryland, someone he would have killed if he had been a little more drunk.

"Men, listen up," said the lieutenant.

Jeremiah moved to the back of the boat to let the officer take his place. His eye caught a turkey buzzard gliding gracefully over the stern, giant wings wavering in the river breeze. It took him back to the day after he lost Messiah along the Yazoo. Just north of Jackson he came upon a group of buzzards tearing apart a fawn carcass in a field. The black vultures hissed, shook their red heads, then urinated as they scattered into the air. In moments they filled the sky, soaring, rising in the draft of hot air flowing up from the newly plowed field. He never forgot how the repellent creatures, with their beady eyes, oily bald heads and urine soaked feet were transformed into images of beauty once they took to the heavens.

"Men, we're near the end of our journey." The lieutenant paused, not so much to be sure he had everyone's attention as to settle himself.

"Take a good look ahead, that's Pea Patch Island..." He turned and pointed, to deepen the effect of his words. "There's mostly Rebs there, over 12,000 by last count." The lieutenant took note of the men's response, a tightening of the hands on the rifle stocks, a thinning of the lips. All eyes focused on the marshy island. "I can tell you no more until we set foot on the dock..."

"How long, Captain," Jeremiah asked, moving back to the front, "how long fur we be der?" The breeze flowing across his face, the soft light jumping off the water, the slick sound of the hull cutting through the chop felt like freedom, and for a moment the sadness in his eyes left, swept up in the crisp autumn air.

"At least a half hour, Sergeant, the tide is turning against us, let's hope the wind doesn't shift to the north." The skipper dribbled some spit on his forefinger and pushed it into the wind. "Once we come abreast of Hamburg Cove, it'll be another twenty minutes. Lower your heads gentlemen we're coming about." The sails filled with a sharp snap, the heavy boom just missing the lieutenant's head. River water splashed across the back of Jeremiah's hand. He licked it then spit the briny liquid back over the side.

"Lotta birds out der, Captain." Jeremiah pointed to waves of starlings weaving back and forth over the island.

"More than you can imagine, Sergeant, the heronry is one of the largest in America, wading birds everywhere ya look."

"Reminds me a Virginia, Captain. Las' year when we be fightin' long de James River, a Reb cannon spooked hundreds a Blue Herons into de air... mos' beautiful thing ever."

"Well, Sergeant, you may meet your feathered friends again."

"How ya mean?"

"The wading birds come up here in the spring from the Carolinas and Virginia to set up and fledge their young...you might say there's a lot more than 12,000 Southerners here." The captain started to laugh but stopped when he saw the soldiers weren't joining in. "Look along the shoreline, just past the sawgrass and the blueberry bushes, about thirty feet up in the trees."

Jeremiah had missed it before. He could see it now, hundreds of large nests, some trees had five or six, all made of intertwined branches.

"You married, Sergeant?"

"No, Captain...I too young for dat."

"Well, the great blue heron has some excellent mating habits." Again the captain fought to keep a straight face. "They're monogamous creatures, nesting pairs...we humans could probably learn a thing or two." This time the captain laughed and the men joined in. "The female picks her husband and mating starts right quick."

"How long, Captain?"

He pulled hard on the rudder to keep the sails trimmed. "Won't be more than five minutes now, best get yourselves ready."

James Bacon had come a long way since his graduation day in Princeton. One-time lawyer, two-time slave master, he had traveled south at the start of the Mexican War to offer his services and fought with such distinction he ended up a major. His bravery at the Battle of Chapultepec misled him into a sense of invulnerability, for in 1848, not long after the war ended, he was seriously wounded in a duel. The only notable fact that came out of that misguided affair was his choice of Thomas J. Jackson as his second. Soon after, he found himself out of the Army and back in the Maryland slavery business. But, in 1859, he returned to the army where he served with moderate success until the beginning of the Rebellion in 1861.

Eager to fight with the Confederates, he resigned his commission and joined up with his old Mexican War comrades in the Fourth Texas Infantry. By mid-1862 he had found his winning rhythm again and was promoted to brigadier general in the Army of Northern Virginia where his brigade won many accolades. This all came with a great cost and by the time his brigade approached Gettysburg, in July of 1863, the general was worn out, a sick man forced to lead his troops from the back of a wagon.

"General, sir, scouts report Yanks ahead."

"Probably just a patrol, Major, I'll be damned if we'll ever find their army."

"No, sir, it's more than a patrol, pickets spotted at least a regiment dug in on a ridge near Gettysburg."

"Have ya tested them?"

"Sir, the Union force hasn't made contact, our pickets held back waiting your direction...it may only be a cavalry unit, hard to tell."

General Bacon put his hands on the wagon floor and pushed forward until his feet touched the ground. "This is no way to fight a war, Major...help me up." Bacon was still a handsome man with a black beard and full mustache. His features were finely cut, and with his aquiline nose he looked younger than his forty-eight years. "It's my leg...gone to sleep on me, Major."

"Here, sir, hold my arm...maybe you should stay in the wagon."

"I appreciate your concern, just stay by me 'til I get some blood back in the leg."

"We could send our skirmishers around to the left, see if there's more to it."

"No, we'll go straight at 'em. I expect them Yanks will turn like the rest of the units we've run down this month."

"I reckon you have that right, sir, show 'em some steel an' they'll be skedaddlin' right quick, hollerin' and cryin' all the way."

"They keep coming back for a-whuppin don't they now?" The general put his hand back to steady himself on the wagon then motioned to his first sergeant. "Contact General Heth, tell him we're probing forward into Gettysburg."

"Very well, I'll await your final orders."

"One more thing, Major, how's the artillery?"

"How ya mean, sir?"

"The iron guns, they gonna hold?"

"I'm told some been fired over 300 times."

"Have those pulled, you know better...one of them cracks it won't be pretty!"

"Yes, sir, I'll have three of the bronze Napoleons brought forward."

"Excellent, Major, my eye prefers the shiny bronze." The general shifted back to his good leg. "Bit steadier now, leg's almost back in order." He took a few steps forward and smiled. "Now get moving...and tell the boys to give an extra yell for me, maybe the Yanks will run before I get up to Gettysburg." The major saluted and turned back to his mount.

"Beautiful horse you got there, Major."

"Yes, sir, she's a Tennessee Walker, smoothest gait in the army I'm sure."

"You best be going, I'll be up soon." A corporal helped the general onto the front wagon seat and they moved off toward the brigade front.

"What's this road, son?"

"Chambersburg Pike, sir, once we cross that creek we'll be back near the brigade." The corporal whistled then pulled back on the reins just enough to steady the wagon so he could point ahead. "Captain tells me there's a low ridge over there just beyond the trees with a Seminary sitting nice an' purty on top. Leave it to the damn Yanks ta set up by a school of God." He crossed himself then kissed his hand. "Look thar, through the trees, just across from our men, that's where dem Yanks are dug in, a rag-tag group fur sure." He wiggled his nose, sniffed the air then cupped his ear. "General, ya hear that?"

"Sounds like the men are eager ta move...can't ask for better than them Tennessee and Alabama boys now can ya?"

"Yes, sir, they're yelling real good for ya!"

"Damn fine fighters, they'll clear them bastards out in no time."

"Best ta turn off here, I'll bring the wagon up to the right." The crackle of musket fire echoed through the woods. Stray balls snapped through the air like angry wasps, exploding tree leaves, snapping branches. Stray artillery rounds thudded into the ground then rolled past, sending up clouds of mosquitoes and an occasional crow. The rich smell of the cut earth was a reminder that it was summer planting season back home. The corporal sneezed, wiped his sleeve across his face, then pulled up a hundred yards behind the Confederate line.

"Look, sir, here comes the major."

"It's Buford's cavalry," cried out the major as he galloped up. "No infantry in sight...y'all best get down, artillery's gonna open up."

"How the numbers look, Major?"

"Just some light artillery and a brigade of dismounted horse soldiers...we should run 'em good." The major turned and pointed toward the Seminary. "Our first line of pickets are about halfway there...should we begin?" He stood up in his stirrups and scratched a sore on his buttocks.

"Pass me your binoculars, Major."

"Here, sir, look just below the Seminary building. Don't look like the Yanks have much ta offer."

Bacon took the field glasses, scanned across the meadow and into the trees. There was still some mist in the humid air. It gave the distant objects a blue cast. "Damn fine optics, Major, I can see a Yankee sniper hiding behind a stump. Look at him now, all purty in his green sharpshooter coat." He held the binoculars away from his eyes and inspected them. "Says they're made in Paris, *Rouge Opticien* inscribed here in the brass."

"Yes, sir, got them off a dead Yank at Fredericksburg...light colonel from the New York Volunteers."

The general scratched a scab on his ear that had been festering since they crossed the Potomac. "Ya right, Major, not much out there, give the order to move the infantry forward, show Buford what Confederate infantry can do when dismounted cavalry stands in their way." He handed the binoculars back and stepped off the wagon. "Yanks are in for a surprise, Major, my only regret is I'm not able to ride out with ya for the whuppin."

The general was so engaged in the scene he seemed unaware of the temperature, but the pickets were already dehydrated. It was just past eight on the first morning of July, 1863. The night had been cool and rainy but a sticky heat settled into the valley soon after the sun rose. The Rebel infantry suffered in long underwear that they hadn't had time to change. The backs of their butternut wool jackets had turned dark from seeping sweat.

"There they go, sir!" A flash of light, then the percussion wave of the Union artillery shook the ground and rippled through the meadow grass. A moment later solid shot whistled by, taking off several treetops but entirely missing the rebel troops. "Must be cavalry, General, aiming them guns high."

"It's a good sign, Major, push the rest of the brigade forward without delay."

"Indeed I shall." The major saluted, spurred on his mount and disappeared into the artillery smoke. The first volley of Confederate muskets ripped the air.

"Perhaps we should back off a little, sir, not my favrit place ta be standing." The corporal was the headquarters company mail clerk and driver. When he wasn't delivering letters his job was to provide transportation for the brigade commanders. A month earlier a colonel on his wagon was cut in half by a stray round. It wasn't just the gore and exploding entrails he feared, the truth was he had come to like the general and didn't relish seeing him exposed to serious injury or death. "I'll pull up the wagon for ya, sir."

The general waved him off. "Ain't no call for that, son, the view's much too good here, warms my heart to see our battle flags moving in good order toward the Yanks." Like most commanders, Bacon ignored the dangers of the battlefield, but it was the wrong day for carelessness.

The corporal could smell trouble, he sensed a shift, saw the problem in time to save his general. "Please, sir, we should retire to the rear."

"Settle down, Corporal, that dog won't hunt." He motioned him back. "Keep the horses calm, I'm enjoying this."

The zip of musket balls now started to mix in with more artillery rounds, punching through the air around the wagon, kicking up dirt. Still the general held his place, sure that the flying ordnance was not permitted to strike him. But, it hit one of their horses. A minnie ball struck the hind leg just below the knee. The projectile didn't just smash into the bone, it exploded half the leg with a pop splash.

"Son a bitching Yanks," cursed the general. "Look at that…just can't be!" The corporal sensed it, but the general saw it first, the forward motion of the Rebel flags wavered then turned.

Desperate to save his commander, the corporal grabbed his arm. "Sir, with respect, I do believe we mus' move back."

Wait!" snapped Bacon, not sure whether to pay attention to the battle or the corporal. The general had a lot to think about. Artillery rounds tumbled past at an alarming rate, solid shot now mixed in with canister and shell. Most ominously, the sound and smell of the fight changed.

"Listen, sir, their shots comin' too fast, our boys don't stand a chance."

"Damn, Corporal, just when I thought we licked 'em." Bacon squinted and tried to see what the Yanks were firing, but the smell in the air told the story. Buford's Union cavalry had the Sharps carbine. The faster firing weapon heated up rapidly and filled the air with a sharp metallic odor like a hot stove. It was nothing like the sweet gunpowder smell of the Confederate muzzleloaders.

"I'll be damned, them motherfuckers got the Sharps, don't they now?"

"Sir, look, Union infantry." The corporal pointed toward the Seminary where a wave of infantry was passing through the Union cavalry line and advancing into the path of the Rebel pickets.

"Git ya ass down, Corporal," yelled the general. "Volley coming..."

He lunged toward the driver and pushed him into a shallow depression near the wagon an instant before thousands of lead balls cut through the grass. The wagon exploded in a shower of splinters. A coarse spray of horse flesh and bone splashed across their uniforms, coating their faces in a bloody mucus smelling of feces.

"Ya all right, sir?"

"Can't see!" Bacon wiped at his eyes but the sticky debris on his hands only made it worse.

"Here, sir, let me help." The corporal took a cloth and started to wipe the general's face.

"Damn mess, what the hell's stuck in my forehead."

"Looks like little pieces of bone sir, all over me too." The corporal spit on the cloth and tried to wipe his commander's eyes. "Don't think ya hurt, sir, jus blood everywhere...here now, try to open ya eyes."

Bacon opened one eye, blinked, then tried the other. "Corporal, can't see right, don't make sense." There was no reply.

"Corporal...Corporal?" The general wiped his eyes again, took another look, but now the view of the field was gone, replaced by a wall of Yankee infantry.

"What the hell, Corporal, where ya at!" He reached out to feel for his driver but there was nothing but wood fragments, mud and bone shards.

"Hey, Lieutenant," said a Yankee private, "lookie what we got here, some kind a big shot..."

"Lieutenant?" called out the general, "shit man...who's there... where's my corporal?"

"My oh my," said the private, "I'll be damned, we have us a Con-Fed-Rat general, look at all dem stars!"

"Let me see...well yes, so we do, never seen such a thing...reckon you just got yourself the biggest catch of the war, Private!"

"What the hell we supposed to do with a Reb general…shoot his Johnny ass?"

"Steady, Private, I'll call the captain, he'll know what to do."

Pea Patch Island - Fall 1863

Jeremiah looked toward the island, now only a stone's throw off the bow. He was twenty-eight years old and numb with fear. More than half a life as a slave, months on the run, and the violence of military service had brought him to this place. He kept his fear hidden, but it left him half sick, his gut wound in tight knots. He imagined his father would have played it safe and stayed on the boat, but that wasn't what Jeremiah signed up for. Better to think of his mother, she'd have marched right off the boat and looked for someone to help. So he stood.

The captain nodded across the water. "We'll be putting in at that dock there, Sergeant, get your men ready."

"Go ahead." The postman bowed and moved aside. "I'll be dropping my bags on the dock, ya'll go first."

"Ya needing a hand?" said Jeremiah.

"No thanks, my postal clerk died on the island last week, I'm offloading the mail and leaving." He pointed at a flatboat tethered to the pier. "It's no place to be."

"Look way too peaceful ta me," whispered Bear. "Where da Rebs?"

"There in that flatboat, there's your Confederates," the postman replied, then spit in the river. "They ran out of luck, been better taking their chances on the battlefield."

Union soldiers with cotton masks and leather gloves dragged long canvas bags off a wagon and rolled them into the hold of the flatboat.

"That's enough of that," said the lieutenant. "Form up the squad, Sergeant." He pushed past the postman and grabbed the rope thrown into the boat by a dock worker. "Move it men, time to stand on some steady ground."

"Ya heard da lieutenant, git ya black asses up da dock."

The masked soldiers struggled with each bag, some rolled easily into the flatboat, others made a thump when a skull or elbow banged against the deck rails.

The lieutenant gestured to the left toward a sandy bank covered with Phragmites reeds. "Sergeant, form up over there."

Jeremiah led the way then knelt in front of the squad and waited for the lieutenant.

"I be 'fraid, Sergeant," said Private Bear, "where all dese dead Rebs coming from?"

Jeremiah looked into the eyes of each of his men and saw the same raw fear that sat in his own gut. His mind turned, searching for a way to calm himself, looking for a way out. "Dear Jesus, who will help us?" he whispered, then he knew.

"Private...ya heard a Harriet Tubman?"

"Course I did..."

"Been four years, almost five since she took me ta Canada," he said, holding one hand to his chest. "Lor know she kept me safe from da marshals."

"Ya be lucky ta see her..."

"She turned me good, promist I be saved. If not fur her I neber leave Canada." Jeremiah glanced to see if the lieutenant was coming. "Soon Lincoln freed us, I come quick ta put on dis uniform." He looked down. A dragonfly sat on his sleeve, it's iridescent wings trembling in the wind. "Now ya listen ta me good...I looked in dat women's eyes an' I see da Lord coming ta save us." He stood, looked at each man, then spoke in barely a whisper, "Every day I remember her an feel der be hope."

"I pray ya speakin' true, Sergeant..."

Jeremiah looked away for a moment, out over the water, focused on the long view to the east, toward Jersey, then put his hand on Bear's shoulder. "Ya not be skeered, Private, dats what I'm tellin' ya."

In the shallows a Great Egret waded out through the eelgrass. The bird turned his head sideways and down, looking for fish, while a Glossy Ibis poked her way through the blueberry bushes on the dunes. Soft afternoon light flowed across the water, bathing the scrub oak leaves in emerald light. "At ease, men," ordered Jeremiah. "Sit down...relax your-selves, der be plenty time to worry later." He sat back against the beach grass, squeezed his eyes shut, sank his fingers into the warm sand.

"Here come de lieutenant, Sarge."

"OK, men, everyone up," said the lieutenant. "Welcome to Pea

Patch Island."

Bear raised his hand, "Where da Rebs, sir, look mighty quiet, thought we be shootin' our way in?"

"Over there," began the lieutenant, pointing toward a large stone fortress just over the dunes.

"How ya mean, sir?"

"It's different here...the enemy has no weapons." The lieutenant paused to watch the reaction, then nodded to Jeremiah.

"This be a prison," said Jeremiah, surprised the lieutenant had turned to him, disappointed he had to reveal he knew what the others didn't. The men stared at Jeremiah then at the lieutenant.

"A prison?" asked Bear. "Ain't we here ta fight Rebs?"

"Like I said, it's a fight...a different kind of fight." The lieutenant reached down, brushed some sand off his pants then broke off a dead branch from a bayberry bush. "Look here, this is where we are." He scratched a map in the sand with the stick. "Just down the road is Fort Delaware, you can see it there, the stone building just over the dunes. High-ranking Confederate officers are kept inside, the others in wood barracks outside the fort."

"So what da fight, dey prisoners or not?"

"Truth is, we're here to relieve the detachment guarding the fort. You see how few we are. There are hundreds of officers waiting in the fort." He motioned to the left of the building. "Over there, there's more... thousands of Rebs...outside."

"What da hell, can't be dat many Johnnies at Delaware?"

"Military command's been sending them from all over, even some of Stonewell Jackson's troops from the Battle of Kernstown. The fight..." the lieutenant hesitated, looked to Jeremiah, "it's not about who's here but the conditions...too many folks for a small island."

"We be relieving da 19th New York Volunteers," said Jeremiah, then sneezed. "They los half der men since May." He turned to find the tree producing the oily scent of heated pine sap that itched his nose.

"If dese Rebs be prisoners, how dey kilt da New York men?"

"No one be fighting," Jeremiah said, then looked back toward the dock where the flatboat was pulling out onto the river with its morbid cargo. "The enemy need no guns...Yanks and Rebs die jus da same." He pointed toward the Jersey shore, where another flatboat was unloading. The afternoon light played tricks with the men's eyes, the distant flatboat seemed to float three feet above the surface of the water. "Jersey, dat's where all de bodies end up, Union and Reb ta gether...ground be too wet here to bury 'em."

The lieutenant squinted, looked at his men, considered how best to break the news. "It's disease, men...enemy here is disease, it's a fight against smallpox, malaria, scurvy, typhoid fever and God knows what."

*For what is your life? It is even a vapour, that appeareth
for a little time, and then vanisheth away.*

JAMES 4:14

FORT DELAWARE - FALL 1863

The last three months had been horrific for James Bacon. Mostly he prayed for death, surely a better place than the living hell he and his men had endured. Falling into the hands of the Yankees at Gettysburg started a chain of events that no general officer in the war had yet experienced. It began with the abject humiliation of capture by a Union private. James could still see the surprise in the soldier's eyes when he saw the rank of the officer he had taken into custody.

Humiliation can be dealt with, can be reasoned into a lesser place, even forgotten after a while. Likewise, his memory of the brutal march of prisoners across Pennsylvania and Maryland in scalding summer heat had faded with time. What he could not bear were the inhuman conditions, the daily burden served up to his men on Pea Patch Island. Compared to his troops he had it good, living within the protective walls of Fort Delaware. His men lived in shabby wooden prison barracks or on the ground around the fort.

Each day he was brought to the ramparts for exercise and there he witnessed the grim life outside the fort. From the high vantage point James saw the meadows and marshes for what they were, the perfect home for water birds and biting insects, but a nightmare for humans. The island, less than one hundred acres in size, was mostly marsh, wet and spongey in all directions. Only the area around the fort was consistently above high tide and even there the sandy soil was damp due to river water seepage below the surface.

The wooden prison barracks were little more than shabby huts. Spaces between the wall boards let in rain, heat, cold and copious swarms of mosquitoes, wasps and rats. The interiors were dank and musty, better suited for the spiders and centipedes that thrived in the damp spaces under the floorboards. The prisoners struggled to sleep on moldy beds, and waged continuous battles with upper respiratory infections and worse. The men inside were covered in lice, while the prisoners living on the grass had to contend with ticks and the dreaded chiggers. Some called them berry bugs but to most they were scrub-itch mites, known for the fearsome holes they produced in the skin followed by nasty irritation and swelling.

Officers inside the fort had three meals a day and the opportunity to hire negroes to cook and do laundry. In view of his high rank, James had been permitted to bring one of his former slaves into the fort to tend to his needs, but that was the exception.

Outside the fort, food was always on the minds of the men because there was so little. James too often saw his men fighting over rodents trapped under the barracks then salted and fried. They endured two sparse meals a day, usually stale bread or hardtack and a tiny piece of boiled grizzle and watery soup. The boiled water in the soup was safe, but not the drinking water. Cases of dysentery and diarrhea spiked as a result. James watched a sergeant waste away until he weighed less than a hundred pounds.

And so, in the midst of all this, General James Bacon found himself approaching his forty-ninth birthday.

"General, I made a cake for ya."

"My goodness, Hany, now you have performed a miracle!"

"Yassuh, a miracle indeed, da New York Volunteers took pity and give us a sack a old cornmeal," she said, then held the cake just below the general's nose. "Forgive me, dis cake smell good but it be low...deres no leavening and but a touch a salt..."

"Please, you mustn't apologize, your presence is my one bright light."

"Massa, ya most kind..." She looked away, the sound of a knock at the door so early in the morning was unexpected. "I putting de cake away, if it be dat fat major from Connecticut he find good 'scuse to share it with his Yankee friends."

"Here, hide it under my bed, I'll answer the door." James pointed toward the bedroom then moved as slow as possible to answer the knock. "You stay put, don't let them know you're in there." The knock came again, louder this time.

James threw the latch and swept the door open as if that would make up for his slow response.

"Good morning..." he began, before he saw who was there.

"Or good afternoon is it...thought maybe you'd died, General?"

"Ah yes, Colonel, do come in." James stepped back and saluted. "Haven't seen ya out here since August."

Hany scrunched tighter into the closet and prayed the colonel would leave. Her experience with most Yankees hadn't been good and the colonel had been rude to her on several occasions.

"General, I've come from Washington with doctors to help contain the smallpox, it's going bad."

"Worse'n bad, Colonel, I've lost twenty men from the regiment this week, and it's not just the pox...we need medicine...castor oil and Epsom salts for the shits, more quinine for malaria." James brushed back his hair to hide his agitation. "Damnation, Colonel, it's a holy mess here, my men are grinding marsh grass to make gruel...that's just not right!"

"General, I hear ya." He scratched his crotch out of nervous habit. "There's just too many men. Maybe we could have handled three thousand prisoners, but we're up to twelve thousand since Gettysburg."

"Open your damn nose, take a good whiff...for God's sake this whole island's a crap hole!"

"Easy now, General, we're doing our best." He rolled his head back and took a quick sniff of the room then reached for his hankie. "Smells like they just flushed out the cesspools of hell now don't it?"

James looked down, didn't want to talk any more but he had to ask, "how many, Colonel...how many have we lost?"

"Getting near two thousand. It's bad enough with the scurvy and dysentery but the pox is raging." The colonel removed his hat and scratched an insect bite on his chin.

"My God man, all you give them is a blanket, a thin coat and watery soup filled with worms...how ya expect them to survive the winter?"

"Can't be sure what's next, been burying hundreds a week over in

Jersey at Finn's Point...pray to God it's a warm winter."

James had nothing more to say, he wanted none of the Yankee nonsense. The muscles tightened in his face, his calves began to cramp.

"Wish I could help, General, but I've come about something else. As you probably heard we've rotated in a new company for garrison duty." He turned his head and gestured to his left. "I've brought their commander and sergeant to meet you."

James figured what this was all about. The new company leaders wanted to establish a good working relationship with the enemy general so it would go easier for them. Fine, he thought, just keep your Yankee hands off my cake.

"This is Lieutenant Barton." A young Union officer stepped from behind the colonel and saluted. The general disliked him immediately. He looked green, right out of school, like he had never seen combat and, from the startled look in his eyes, he certainly had never met a Reb.

The general saluted. "At ease, Lieutenant, I won't bite ya." He started to laugh but immediately choked it back as the next Yankee stepped forward.

"This is my sergeant."

Jeremiah did not move forward. He had thought about this first moment with a Confederate and dreaded it. His body language expressed the loss and abuse he had suffered. He could not hide his disdain. He moved slowly in front of the general and saluted without looking up.

"I'm General Bacon, where ya from, Sergeant?" James felt weak, the first twinge of nausea gripped his gut. He had never seen a black soldier before, didn't know there could be such a thing. He tried his best but the insincerity was palpable. Not only was he faced with a black soldier but there was something unsettling about his looks, something familiar and strange at the same time.

Back in the bedroom it was an entirely different matter. Hany knew revealing herself would greatly displease the general but something was amiss and one way or another she was coming out. She pushed the cake further under the bed with her foot and squinted. She could not see the men at the door but the voices were clear. Hany began to shake. Beads of perspiration appeared on her forehead, a pounding in her chest started to rise beyond a level she could endure. One foot moved forward, then another.

"I be born in Mary's Land," Jeremiah replied. He had to say it that way, it made him feel better, took the fear out of his stomach, gave him the courage to raise his head. He looked the general in the eye.

"Where, Sergeant?"

"Perry...Perry..." Jeremiah never stuttered and certainly was no mumbler, but he could not form the words. His cheek muscles trembled so hard he could not move his lips into the proper shape to say the word.

"Perry Town!" cried out Hany. "Praise de Lord."

Jeremiah and the colonel stepped back, startled by the mysterious outburst from the bedroom. The general's face turned red.

"Precious Jesus, could dis be ma boy!" Hany was moving now, out of the dark. "Hell with da cake," she whispered.

Jeremiah turned toward the woman. "Mama...Hany?" He started towards her but the general caught him, held him at arm's length.

"Hany?"

She pulled up halfway across the room to listen to the way he said her name. She knew it was Jeremiah, her body told her, the choking wave of tightness in her chest, the stinging wet in her eyes.

*Why have I not fallen with my contemporaries, the end
of an exhausted race? Why do I alone remain to seek their
bones in the dust and dark of a crowded catacomb?*

FRANCOIS-RENE DE CHATEAUBRIAND

Coda

The vagaries of history and the distance of time have not been kind to poor folk, especially former slaves of the antebellum era. Hearsay, and very little of it, is all that remains of Hany and Jeremiah's story. For a Confederate general there is more to tell. James Bacon was eventually released in a prisoner exchange. He left Fort Delaware in June of 1864 and by late summer the general was back with his original brigade in the Army of Northern Virginia.

The war had changed dramatically since Gettysburg. Not only did the Union forces have the rebels on the run, but more ominously for James Bacon, the tactics themselves had changed. It had become a war of attrition with armies facing each other in static positions. The generals had at last determined that massed headlong attacks into the face of a well positioned enemy with modern weaponry were suicidal. Even the aggressive General Grant expressed regret for his disastrous charge at Cold Harbor.

Trench warfare was the new face of war and it was in a series of muddy dugouts before Petersburg, Virginia that General Bacon found himself after leaving Fort Delaware. In his weakened condition, from months of exposure to disease, insects and the weather extremes of prison, the trenches were the last place he belonged. He needed a hospital or at least a quiet respite, certainly not the rain-slick entrenchments of a siege. The trenches, which afforded a good measure of safety from small arms fire and stray artillery rounds, were perfect traps for filth and garbage. It was only because of the mortal danger above that anyone dared stay in their fetid bottoms. It took neither weeks nor months for them to have their effect on James Bacon. Within days of his entrance into the foul atmosphere, he was fighting a fever of 104 degrees and by early October was laid to rest in Richmond.

Our story would have ended there, in the cold earth of Hollywood Cemetery, but for one unexpected discovery. The general's staff, when preparing his body for burial, removed his muddy battle uniform and found, in his ripped breast pocket, a diary. It was not the typical hardbound diary but rather a sheaf of torn foolscap bound with a piece of twine. James had become an avid writer while in prison and all we know of Jeremiah and Hany comes from that diary. There is nothing else, neither town records, letters or family history to fill in the blanks:

PEA PATCH ISLAND ~ August 17, 1863

...much too hot to sleep...the ferocious smell of the field latrines outside my window makes me nauseous...it permeates everything, my clothes smell like garbage, the food tastes of shit...I hardly eat anymore...one bit of good news, the adjutant has come to tell me I can bring a slave from home if she will help cook in the mess...

PEA PATCH ISLAND ~ September 1, 1863

...imagine, Hany has been sent here by my mother...such a good surprise...she made her way back to our plantation after her owner's property in Virginia was destroyed by a Union raiding party and now she is with me...

PEA PATCH ISLAND ~ September 3, 1863

...the pox took five more of my men...two of them suffered for a month with scurvy before the disease grabbed them...they died three days later...I go out when I can to be with my men...the guards tell me to stay away from the infected but I'm not afraid...

PEA PATCH ISLAND ~ September 9, 1863

...Hany was quite nervous at first, even with me, but now she has settled in and is cooking with the white women...it has rained for three days and everything made from cloth, even my bedding, is damp and musty...the brick walls of our rooms are slick with green mold...I lie awake fighting headaches...

PEA PATCH ISLAND ~ September 11, 1863

...writing of death over and over leaves me exhausted...desperation drove me to ask Hany to do the impossible and try to save my men using variolation...the slaves carried the technique with them from Africa...I insisted she try it on me first...she snuck into the morgue late last night and scraped a scab off one of my men who had died of the pox...she then opened a small cut on my arm with her paring knife and poked part of the scab under the skin...

PEA PATCH ISLAND ~ September 23, 1863

...the rash on my face and forearm has spread to my stomach...the fever has been mild, not the delirious malady experienced by most... the lesions have started to harden, they feel like little stones under my skin...I pray I will survive...

PEA PATCH ISLAND ~ September 26, 1863

...better today...I talked to my men and offered Hany's services but only a few accepted the procedure...I'm not sure if it was fear of the disease or of a slave cutting them, but worse for those who declined...I can smell the sea in the breeze tonight, it washes out the foulest of the odors from the latrines...maybe I will sleep tonight...

PEA PATCH ISLAND ~ September 28, 1863

...one of the white cooks caught her dress on fire cooking breakfast at the big stoves...Hany smothered her in a blanket, saved her life, but the poor woman suffers from burns on her arms...the mess sergeant has put Hany in charge of the kitchen, he can see as well as I that

she is a safer cook, knows how to wrap her dress when she is near the stoves...her food is a damn sight better than the trash served by the Yankee cooks...the guards love her apple pie, she makes the crust with bacon grease...

PEA PATCH ISLAND ~ September 30, 1863

...had a long talk with Hany this afternoon after her kitchen chores were done...she cried in my arms when I tried to apologize for selling her...never held a slave before, seems so strange that I did such a thing, never apologized to anyone about anything before...she has changed my life here and I had to say I was sorry, for my own peace of mind...prison changes the way you see things...

PEA PATCH ISLAND ~ October 2, 1863

...first cold patch since spring, my men stayed in their barracks until late afternoon...there was no frost, but with a steady wind coming in from the ocean the smaller birds seemed to know it was time to head south...there was a beautiful thrush with tan eye rings and pink legs that came to my window all summer...he's gone now...last night I dreamed General Lee invaded Washington and captured Lincoln...

PEA PATCH ISLAND ~ October 6, 1863

...a miracle has occurred...Jeremiah came to my door like a phantom from another world...I was so numb you could have struck me dead... and he, now a Union sergeant...I am sure that what I had suspected for months is true: the world has turned upside down and if I survive, my former life will no longer exist...

PEA PATCH ISLAND ~ October 9, 1863

...Jeremiah passes by often but will not speak...and Hany has changed...she avoids me, does only what is required...the major lets her eat lunch with Jeremiah when their duties permit...I wish to say so much to them but I leave it alone...the weather has turned mild again...more men died of dysentery than small pox this week...we are surrounded by sickness and death, it leaves me afraid and depressed... sleep comes in spurts, mostly I lie awake until first light then sleep for

an hour before breakfast...

PEA PATCH ISLAND ~ October 10, 1863

*...I think often of the moment a few days ago when Jeremiah ap-
peared out of nowhere...I had no idea who he was...he stood there
with his head down...I was terribly uncomfortable but thought it
was because he was a Negro soldier...he must have recognized me...
there was a powerful surge of emotion that seemed to enter my being but still I didn't understand...it was as if the sadness of another
world had penetrated my soul...then suddenly, when he spoke, my
mind cleared and the terrible pain began...I seemed to have moved
on the other side of a wall and may never return...*

PEA PATCH ISLAND ~ November 2, 1863

*...three more of my men tried to escape yesterday...surely it's a sign of
desperation, not common sense...the river water is so frigid no one
could last for long in the swirling currents...one of them washed up
on the beach near the dock today, another was fished out of the water
by the arriving packet boat...God only knows what became of the
third...*

PEA PATCH ISLAND ~ November 15, 1863

*...it has been nearly four months since I came here...my weight has
dropped below 140 pounds...I saw my face reflected in a window and
did not recognize myself...*

PEA PATCH ISLAND ~ November 19, 1863

*...Hany is sick...she has left the kitchen and been isolated in one of the
magazine lockers under the fort...no one is allowed to see her until
they determine if she has the pox...*

PEA PATCH ISLAND ~ November 28, 1863

*...today we awoke to the first dusting of snow...our rooms are AL-
WAYS cold...I fear for Hany in this weather...she is wasting away,
shivering and sweating, perhaps from something in the foul water...I*

visit her when permitted, usually after dinner...the kitchen without Hany has returned to the inedible slop of the white cooks but at least they allow me to eat near the stove...Jeremiah still avoids me...

PEA PATCH ISLAND ~ December 15, 1863

...I pray to God that somehow I can be forgiven for the grievous harm I have caused Hany and Jeremiah...she is near death, there can be no hope she will survive...I read to her every night from the Old Testament, most often passages from Solomon's Song, her favorite book: My beloved spake, and said unto me, Rise up, my love, my fair one, and come away. For lo the winter is past, the rain is over and gone; The flowers appear on the earth; the time of the singing birds is come, and the voice of the turtle is heard in our land...let me hear thy voice; for sweet is thy voice...

PEA PATCH ISLAND ~ December 25, 1863

...Hany passed last night...Jeremiah was with her...it was a bone chilling vigil, even more so in her small chamber below the fort... it never seemed like Christmas Eve, only when the dinner cooks reminded me did I know...my thoughts then went back to my first Christmas home after I left Princeton...what a sweet moment it was, full of love and family warmth...I could hardly look at Hany thinking of it...God have mercy on us all...

PEA PATCH ISLAND ~ December 27, 1863

...Hany was taken to the burial site this morning with three of my men, all dead from the pox...they permitted Jeremiah to ride along with the four bodies and a crew of diggers...I watched from the fort's ramparts as the small boat made its way across the choppy waters to Jersey...all were buried as usual in a common grave...Jeremiah did all the digging and filling, wouldn't let anyone else move the earth...

PEA PATCH ISLAND ~ February 17, 1864

...another miracle, Jeremiah has begun to speak to me...his first words were about his mother's burial...how he stepped down into the open grave and took her body from the men above...all he could see when he

looked up was a large sweet gum...wisteria vines encircled the trunk and climbed toward the top where gray catbirds rode the swaying branches...it all reminded him of the Maryland plantation, especially the loamy smell of the exposed earth...he placed a gold coin on each of Hany's eyes then wrapped a long white cotton cloth around her head and kissed her hands...I have no idea how he came to have in his possession such valuable coins, one a five dollar gold piece, the other a twenty...

PEA PATCH ISLAND ~ February 22, 1864

...over the past week Jeremiah told me the story of his life from the day he left the plantation and I have written it all down...there is something about the dark mystery of his journey that gives me hope, exactly because of its futility...

PEA PATCH ISLAND ~ February 28, 1864

...nearly a thousand of our men have died here...for some reason I have been spared...my feet ache from the cold stone floors, not even the kitchen stove can turn them...

PEA PATCH ISLAND ~ March 17, 1864

...the impossible happened tonight, we had a winter thunderstorm... it moderated the raucous Irish celebration that had gone on all evening...It was an Irishman from the Iron Brigade that captured me at Gettysburg, so tonight's celebration did not please me...

PEA PATCH ISLAND ~ March 23, 1864

...Jeremiah's unit rotated out yesterday...he never said goodbye...

ENVOI

Hany lies with 2,346 Confederates in long trenches at Finn's Point National Cemetery. Only Jeremiah would have known her exact location. A tall granite obelisk with bronze markers was raised over the deceased in 1910. The Rebel prisoners are identified in raised letters on green oxidized metal plaques that include each prisoner's name, company and regiment. No slaves are listed. On the opposite side of the cemetery, near the entrance, are the graves of 135 Union Civil War soldiers who died while serving at Fort Delaware and, in the North corner of the lawn, not far from the Confederate obelisk, are the marked tombs of 11 Nazi prisoners who died at Fort Dix during World War II.

The fates of Hany and James Bacon are part of history. What became of Jeremiah is unknown, we will never have it. He disappeared into the great maelstrom of the war and time passed.

A century and a half.

Some say that the pain of war lives on only for the losing side. Today the *Lost Cause* keeps its hold on the old South while the war's turmoil is all but forgotten in the Yankee states. Below the Mason-Dixon line Confederate battle flags spring up periodically, the great rebel generals are honored, the Southern fallen are remembered. In the North there is little of this, and yet, on a small island in the meandering path of the Erie Canal system in Western New York State, a Civil War memorial honors Confederates and Yankees together and in so doing bears a measure of relevance to our story.

Coming from the south, after passing through Ithaca, Route 96 glides through endless corn and wheat fields high above the vineyards lining the shores of Cayuga and Seneca Lakes. On a typical midsummer day temperatures spike into the nineties, the crisp azure sky looms large, high feathery clouds point toward Waterloo. A quick right and left at the edge of town brings the traveler to the canal and Lock Island. The narrow island takes its name from Lock 4 whose blue gates and towers line the south side. Closely cropped lawns spread across the terrain, old growth shade trees and gnarled pine provide texture. Opposite the lock, on the north side, monoliths of limestone and marble rise from the earth. In the middle of the island, near a blood red flagpole flying the American flag of 1865, a cenotaph constructed of thirty-six stones and bricks bakes in the sun. On the northeast corner of the monument is a reddish orange brick sent from the Old Court House Museum in Vicksburg, Mississippi. The brick arrived with its own story.

It seems that in 1863, Admiral David Dixon Porter, aboard the Union flagship *Black Hawk*, spotted the Vicksburg Court House. It seemed the perfect target, especially with the Stars and Bars flying from a pole on the cupola. The Admiral ordered his men to throw shells at the building. Most of the ordnance missed, but one scored a direct hit near the roof line and sent a section of bricks flying.

After the war's end the bricks were gathered and stored in the courthouse basement for repairs. Most were used to patch the building, but a few remained in storage for well over a century. It was from this collection that a brick was drawn for shipment to the American Civil War Memorial in Waterloo. Today it is mortared into the cenotaph with a perfect impression of Jeremiah's thumbprints pressed into the brick's end. Those small relics are all that remain of the man, but surely they mark the moment of hope in a life dominated by loss and servitude. In the midst of oppression he dared to act and in so doing brought a measure of dignity to his life.

> *Had I the heavens' embroidered cloths,*
> *Enwrought with golden and silver light,*
> *The blue and the dim and the dark cloths*
> *Of night and light and the half-light,*
> *I would spread the cloths under your feet:*
> *But I, being poor, have only my dreams;*
> *I have spread my dreams under your feet;*
> *Tread softly because you tread on my dreams.*
>> YEATS

The Sky - Late Fall 2010

From three thousand feet the island doesn't look like much. Except for the pentagonal shape of the fort, Pea Patch Island could be mistaken for a raft of seaweed and sticks floating down river. The heron feathers her wings, floats higher. The north end of the island glows orange in the low angle rays of the sun and the bird imagines she sees her nest, or maybe not, it's just a sandy colored patch from high altitude.

Although the signs are there, the heron does not want to leave. Her mate and young have disappeared. She waited, hoping they would return, hoping the time for the long flight south had not come, but the lengthening nights and change in the winds could not be ignored. Activity at the fort has ended, boats have stopped arriving from the mainland and lights in the buildings remain dark, sure signs of winter's approach.

Slowly, in great ascending arcs, she climbs higher, seeking the southern wind current that will ease the journey. The sun has set but the glow to the west gives direction. Then she feels it, the tailwind at four thousand feet ruffles her tail, pushes her forward. She looks down, the island now out of focus as the river mists drift across the dunes and marshes. One more turn up and she will fully engage in the river of air. Somewhere ahead, along the path her family took, she will find the winter nest.

A slender crescent moon rests in the chilly air, a reminder that Pisces will rise soon and take her home. One last look, Pea Patch Island now only a faint grey smudge in the water below. Heaven is a hard place to leave.

Acknowledgments

A novel never finds itself wrought into readable form without innumerable edits, comments and suggestions. Nearly one hundred friends and students plowed their way through my drafts and made the story work. Special mention goes to Thomas Baker, my urbane webmaster, great friend and expert martini shaker, who produced this book and read and reread the pages many times. Also to Cathy Vanderpool, my archeologist, whose extensive comments caused me to review the smallest details for historical accuracy. Who would have thought that pesto and linguini could be found in an Italian cookbook published in 1863 or that you could have enjoyed a glass of Chianti in Florence in the early seventeenth century? To Ben Ripley, the real writer in my circle of friends and my Signore who shares a deep love for all things Latin. I'll never forget his advice many years ago when he read the draft of my first attempt at a novel that was a bit long on physical description...*I love your detailed descriptions of the landscape, but Pietro, this is a novel, something has to happen!* To Caren Brenman, Philadelphia poet and writer, whose succinct comments led me in the right direction in the early drafts of *Memorial Day*. To Pat Pickrel, my amazing one-woman legal team, whose interest in the stories encouraged me forward and ceaselessly kept the process moving toward publication. To Ena Barton, my musical muse and classical pianist extraordinaire, and to Michelle Calabro, whose photography of the American Civil War Memorial has shown us new ways of seeing.

The Village of Waterloo is at the center of the story and it is to all the residents and friends I met while working there that I owe my humblest gratitude. Caren Cleaveland, the driving force behind the creation of the American Civil War Memorial, became a dear friend and supporter of all I do. Her home became my home, her singing, building, reenacting, researching and deep respect for the fallen of the Civil War made both the memorial and the novel possible. Right beside her stood Bill Holmes, volunteer supervisor during construction and tireless landscaper beyond compare. Thanks also to Mayor Ted Young and Deputy Mayor/Trustee Dave Duprey, great supporters of the memorial project, and to Ted's wife Judy who saved *The Waterloo Military Record Book*. That primary document was the critical link in tracing the stories of the Waterloo fallen.

Also I give my great thanks to the reenactor and veteran units who have supported the memorial and attend the Waterloo Civil War events. These include the Daughters of Union Veterans, the Sons of Union Veterans, the 148th New York Volunteer Infantry and Reynolds Battery L. Sergeant Jim Goloski of the 148th always looked to me like he stepped right out of a Civil War history book. Anyone who boils eggs in his morning coffee is my kind of soldier. Major thanks to Jim for giving permission to use his image on the cover.

The stories of *Savages Station* saw their birth in the research undertaken by a dedicated group of friends and students. In Waterloo, American Civil War Committee members Caren Cleaveland and Dale Theetge, and volunteer David Calabro, worked with primary and secondary documents to authenticate the lists of the fallen. Frank Varney, who completed his Ph.D. in Civil War History at Cornell in 2008, worked with his students to gather additional information. His book, *General Grant and the Rewriting of History*, was published in 2013. My art student, Erin Byrne, was a junior at the Stuart School in Princeton when she reviewed the military service and pension records in the National Archives (Washington, DC) relating to the Waterloo Fallen. Erin graduated from Princeton University in 2013.

My wife Maria always seems to find herself, sooner or later, in some type of adventure cooked up by her husband. It began in a military chapel at Fort Carson where we were married and more recently involved numerous visits to Civil War sites and many, many military ceremonies. Maria has a way with everyone. Without her I never could have gained access to the places and people that were crucial to the writing of *Savages Station*. Imagine, she even talked her way into the National Archives one night when we were told they were closing! My deepest thanks to the love of my life.

About the Author

Pietro del Fabro is a designer, sculptor and writer. He has completed public art commissions in South Carolina, Virginia, Washington D.C., New Jersey and New York. His interest in the Civil War developed early. He was a United States History major at Hobart College and later served in the U. S. Army Infantry. In 2008 he completed his design for the American Civil War Memorial in Waterloo, NY. Unlike most Civil War Memorials that either pay tribute to the Northern or Southern dead, the Memorial in Waterloo takes a different and singular path - it honors both the Union and Confederate soldiers and sailors lost during America's bloodiest war. The project includes sixty-two sculptures in marble and limestone. The American Civil War Memorial was noted by CBS-TV as a *Top Five Must-See Civil War Era Site in New York State.*

Other major commissions include the West Windsor (NJ) Veterans' Monument (1990) for which he received a citation for meritorious service from the American Legion. In 1993 he received an award from the National Art Honor Society for artistic contributions to the community. He completed a limestone stele for the United States Forest Service in 2005. The stele, which commemorates the four Alaskan leaders who lost their lives at the 2005 Boy Scout Jamboree, is on display at the Washington, D.C. headquarters of the Forest Service. Pietro was a regular contributor to *Environment & Art Letter* (Chicago, LTP) on the subject of Italian Romanesque and Renaissance art and architecture (1994-2005). He also is the author of *Cherubim of Gold*. Visit his studio online: www.pietrodesigns.com.

CPSIA information can be obtained at www.ICGtesting.com
Printed in the USA
BVOW05s0358010516

446188BV00001B/3/P